My So-Called Family

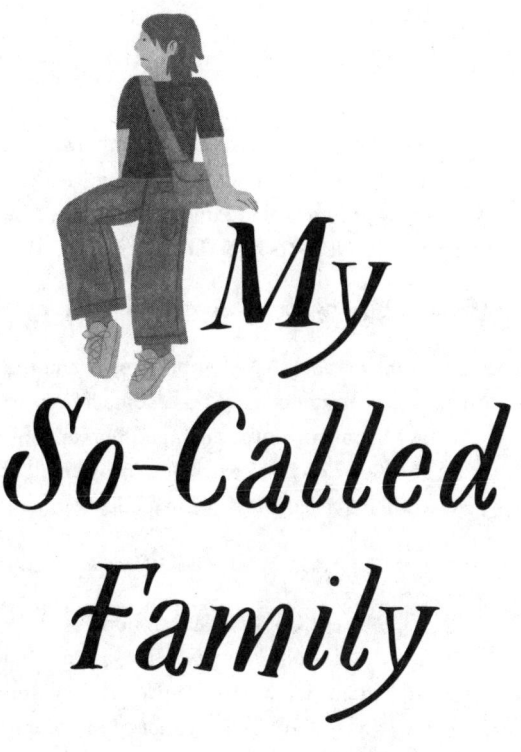

My So-Called Family

Gia Gordon

Farrar Straus Giroux
New York

Farrar Straus Giroux Books for Young Readers
An imprint of Macmillan Publishing Group, LLC
120 Broadway, New York, NY 10271 • mackids.com

Copyright © 2024 by Carrie Gordon. All rights reserved.

Our books may be purchased in bulk for promotional,
educational, or business use. Please contact your local
bookseller or the Macmillan Corporate and Premium Sales Department at (800) 221-7945 ext. 5442 or by email at
MacmillanSpecialMarkets@macmillan.com.

Library of Congress Cataloging-in-Publication Data

Names: Gordon, Gia, author.
Title: My so-called family / Gia Gordon.
Description: First edition. | New York : Farrar Straus Giroux, 2024. | Audience: Ages 8–12. | Audience: Grades 4–6. | Summary: Sixth-grader artist Ash, who has been in foster care most of her life, struggles with an ancestral tree assignment, but soon discovers the true meaning of family.
Identifiers: LCCN 2023043752 | ISBN 9780374392055 (hardcover)
Subjects: CYAC: Middle schools—Fiction. | Schools—Fiction. | Foster home care—Fiction. | Friendship—Fiction. | Belonging—Fiction.
Classification: LCC PZ7.1.G65459 My 2024 | DDC [Fic]—dc23
LC record available at https://lccn.loc.gov/2023043752

First edition, 2024
Book design by Julia Bianchi
Printed in the United States of America by Lakeside Book
Company, Harrisonburg, Virginia

ISBN 978-0-374-39205-5
1 3 5 7 9 10 8 6 4 2

*For Frances Gordon, my mamacita,
who gave me a heart to call home*

My So-Called Family

The Long, Slender Abdomen...

. . . **of Dragonia Volante swishes** menacingly as her enemies cower in fear.

I shall vanquish you all, one by one! she cries.

Except I don't like how her dragonfly wings look. They're too short and stubby. I pull an eraser out of the canvas crossbody I'm wearing. I'm not usually a crossbody kind of girl, but it keeps my art supplies from falling everywhere when I'm up in my private drawing tree.

I lengthen Drago's forewings. That's better. It looks more like her.

I shall vanquish you all—

Slam.

Jordan storms out of the house, gets about halfway to his truck, stops.

"Ashley, get your butt outta that tree," he says without even looking up. "Go help Gladys with the baby."

I roll my eyes. "He's your baby," I whisper, but not loud enough for Jordan to hear. He'd throttle me if he heard me.

"It wouldn't kill you to help with dinner tonight, either, so Gladys doesn't have to do everything," he barks.

"Where are *you* going?" I ask as I scramble down the trunk.

He turns on me, narrows his eyes. "Hold up, do I answer to *you*? Or do you answer to me?"

Neither, I think. *I'm just a kid. I'm not even your kid—I'm your mom's foster. You're the one who's not supposed to be here.*

"Now get in there and finish your homework," he says, "before you flunk out of sixth grade."

Like you flunked out of tenth? I think. Lucky for Jordan, I keep this thought to myself.

And don't call me Ashley either. It's Ash. Just. Ash.

When I get inside, I don't finish my homework.

I finish my drawing.

I draw Jordan in the clutches of Drago, her mandibles open and ready to devour his whole head.

I'm pretty sure no one would even miss him.

Wiz Porter Giggles...

...in third-period English as he passes his phone across the aisle to Matt Adams.

They both look at me.

Now they're both giggling.

I pull my hoodie over my head, slide the strings so they cinch around my face, like Drago's massive portal to her lair—a metal iris with curved, interlocking teeth that opens and closes to keep enemies from entering her secret hideout. My hoodie version kind of does the same.

I stare down at my notebook. My drawing of Dragonia Volante stares back at me. Drago is my superhero alter ego. She's a dragonfly-woman hybrid. She has eight little brothers and sisters who she loves and helps with their homework and stuff, even when they're being bratty to her. She calls out every injustice. She's kind of a boss.

I erase the lines representing waves of destructive power coming from Drago's crystal-clear wings and change the drawing to Drago swiping the phone away from Matt Adams and crushing it in her powerful mandibles. Then I add a picture of her setting Wiz Porter's hoodie on fire with the force of her stare. *That's for telling people you're a wizard!* she says.

Wiz Porter is not a wizard. That's not even his name—it's Alan. I know, because the teachers call "Alan Porter" for roll every day and he mumbles, "Here." But he still tells people his real name is Wiz.

He swears it.

Wiz pops Matt Adams on the arm and tells him to pass the phone to Joss Cruz. Joss smirks at the screen and hands it back.

She says "Grow up" to Matt and Wiz.

But a smirk is still a smile.

She looks at me in between shoving the phone at him and turning back around.

My heart does a thing. That thing.

I mean . . .

That thing it does when Joss Cruz turns around in her seat sometimes.

I don't have a crush on Joss.

That doesn't mean I couldn't have a crush on her. I mostly just like her supreme coolness. She may be the coolest person at school.

"Ashley . . ."

I pop up at the sound of Ms. Kim's voice calling me by the wrong name.

"It's just Ash," I mumble.

"You'll need to pull your hoodie down," she says. "No hats inside."

I run a mental scan of her, the way Drago would. Villain or no? It may be too early in the year to know how I feel about Ms. Kim.

"Matt and Wiz are passing a cell phone," I blurt.

This is not even close to what Drago would say at a moment like this.

Ms. Kim turns, walks toward Matt and Wiz, parks one hand on her hip, holds the other one out toward them. She doesn't say a word as Matt drops the phone into her hand.

"You may see me after class," she tells them.

Okay, well. Maybe I don't for sure know if I like Ms. Kim yet.

But I for sure don't *not* like her.

We Have to Make a Family Tree...

...in social studies. It's only the first week of middle school, and that's the assignment already. Mr. Mann tells us to think of it like a "family dynasty" because that's what we're studying. He can tell us to think about it however he wants, but I still don't have one.

My eyes close in around the words on the board. I draw a partly opened metal iris on my paper. Drago can make the curved spikes of the giant circular portal open and close together on demand, expanding and contracting to keep evildoers from gaining access to her lair. I'm using it to keep the words *family tree* from stabbing me in the heart.

Drago's metal iris is perfect for separating all the kids who have a family from the kid who doesn't.

In my drawing, she uses her wings to keep the iris from closing all the way. Her mouth opens, and she says the words *a family tree*.

a family tree

A family tree isn't the same thing as *your family tree*.

Mr. Mann wrote *a family tree*.

He says, "I want to see at least three generations of a family tree."

I can draw three generations of *a* family tree that isn't *my* family tree. I can do that in my sleep.

Taryn Swisher leans over and *pssssst*s at me.

"Will you draw mine?" she whispers.

"*What?*" I whisper back. I heard what she said. I just want her to get in trouble for asking me to do the assignment for her. That's cheating.

"Will. You. Draw. Mine. For. Me."

"Draw *what* for you?" I say again, way louder than I need to, even to get someone in trouble.

Mr. Mann turns toward me. I can tell he's one of those old cranky types. He's probably forty. I bet he has at least ten grandkids. I bet his grandkids know everything there is to know about their actual family. Not all of us are that lucky.

He says, "What's your name, kiddo?"

"Dalton," I say.

He looks at his roll sheet, going back through the list a couple of times.

"Again?" he says, tapping his ear. "I have a little trouble hearing—too many Anvil of Doom concerts back in the day."

I have no idea what he's talking about, but this

time, I swirl up the words "Ash Dalton" just to confuse him.

"*It's Ashley Dalton*," someone says, loud and clear, from the back of the room.

I spin around. It's hard to tell if it was Chase Williams or that one dude who always wears Aerosmith T-shirts. When we moved to Chico last year, I went to Citrus Elementary with Chase and Wiz and all of them. But I can never remember that other dude's actual name—I just think of him as Steven Tyler, who according to Jordan is Aerosmith's "front man." Jordan loves that band too. He even has some of the same T-shirts. Right now, *this* Steven Tyler is elbow bumping with Chase Williams, so I'm pretty sure one of those guys said it.

"Okay, kiddo," Mr. Mann says to no one in particular. "Keep the outbursts to a minimum, all right? We've got a lot to get through today."

I flip my notebook open and sketch Drago lassoing Chase and Steven Tyler with her mile-long tongue and feeding them to a humungous toad version of our teacher. Cartoon Mr. Mann has warts all over his face and fangy teeth as he writes *Reveal Your Deepest Secrets* on the board. The letters fall like leaves off a family tree.

Nice try, Mr. Mann. I will never reveal my deepest secrets to you. *My* family secret is locked up again for I-don't-know-how-long-this-time, so . . . maybe if my mom ever gets out of prison, I'll do a family tree then. But I'm definitely not gonna make one now.

For now, I decide that I don't like Mr. Mann. He seemed cool on the first day of class, calling everyone *kiddo* because he hadn't learned our names yet and playing icebreakers with us. Even though I'm not always a fan of those let's-get-to-know-each-other activities, I'm woman enough to admit they do help sometimes. Otherwise, I'd probably go a whole school year without talking to anyone in class.

Which, let's be honest.

I'd mostly be fine with that.

The Cafeteria Is a Bad Place to Eat...

. . . but it's a good place to draw.

I open my sketchbook, trying to decide who I'm going to capture today. The kids play-pushing each other? The awkward couples holding hands? The teacher who's been forced to give up her own lunchtime to stand there, leaning up against the stage to watch us during ours?

Gentry Noble plunks down next to me, straddling the seat bench. I can finally exhale, now that my best friend—my only friend, actually—is by my side in the caf. After almost a week of school, the cafeteria still feels like a shaken can of soda someone could pop open at any minute.

"Dude, what are you wearing?" I ask.

He looks down at the green button-up shirt with wide beige stripes and says, "It's my dad's old bowling shirt." Because every day is dress-like-a-rando day for Gentry. "So . . . I assume you haven't seen it?" he adds, pushing his almost-white blond hair out of his face.

That's never a good place to start. No one ever says that when something fantastic has happened.

I go, "Seen what?"

He slides the phone from his pocket, taps out his passcode real quick, opens his photos, and flips it around to show me.

"I screenshotted it."

"Wow," I say when the air starts pumping back into my lungs. When I blink enough times to unblur the doctored image of myself staring up at me. "Someone's getting really good at Photoshop. I don't even *have* those body parts."

"You're not mad?" he asks.

I push his phone out of my face.

"People have been photoshopping pictures of me since I moved here last year. I mean . . . yeah, I'm mad. It always makes me mad. But . . . what am I supposed to do about it?"

"Okay, but none of them were like this," he says.

He's right. I've never been given boy parts before, but there they are—drawn in right over the same basic jeans and T-shirt I always wear. And they've added callouts. *Bieber hair. Flat chest. Walmart boys' department. Peach fuzz.* They put the grossest callout on the parts they drew in. But it doesn't change anything. It doesn't make me want to grow my hair long and put it in a messy bun, or wear dresses, or use makeup, just so some insecure dudes at school can feel more comfortable about how I look. They'd just find something else to drag me for.

We glance around the cafeteria for a few minutes before Gentry goes, "You hungry at all?"

I *am* hungry. But after hearing so many stories about middle school cafeterias being war zones with weaponized food, Gentry and I have been careful about eating in here. Nothing bad has happened yet. Even so, someone could decide they like what *you* brought for lunch more than what *they* brought and just . . . take it.

My stomach growls. "Yeah," I say. "I'm kinda hungry."

I watch him sneak a Twix bar out of his backpack and look around before peeling it open on the stealth. He pushes his hair out of his eyes again, then hands one of the pieces to me before shoving the whole other piece into his mouth all at once. I break my half in half and pretend to cover a yawn so no one can see me eating it. Maybe that's a little extreme—I mean, no one's gonna literally take a candy bar out of your mouth. But I'm still not taking any chances. First, it's Twix bars. Next thing you know, you're getting punched in the face for—

Joss Cruz.

Across the cafeteria, near the tray return.

Eating pepperoni pieces off a slice of pizza.

Discarding the cheese.

Rolling up the soggy crust and eating it like a corn dog.

Her friends laughing at her.

Joss Cruz is so cool, I would draw her panel by panel just so I could study the way her brown-gold hair flips as she throws her head back. How her mouth opens into a wide smile, just before the pepperoni drops in. How she laughs with her whole body after that, since her mouth is full. How her light-brown eyes nearly close whenever she—

"You might want to contain your obvious," Gentry whispers, pulling a ChapStick out of his pocket.

"Huh?"

He cracks a single look in Joss's direction, then whips it back.

"You think eating a Twix in the cafeteria can get you in trouble with Wiz and those guys . . ." He leaves the rest of the understood threat hanging in midair, floating on the greasy smell of Tater Tots. I watch as he rolls up the ChapStick, only it's *not* ChapStick inside. He's made it into a tube of cheese. My mouth drops open as he takes a bite off the top.

"I . . . It wasn't like that," I say. "I was just noticing how . . ." I look over at Wiz and them real quick, then at Joss, then back to Gentry. "How loud those girls are. Jeez."

He nods, but I'm not sure he believes me.

"It's not what you think," I add.

"It doesn't matter what *I* think," he says as the bell rings.

We get up from the table and he goes, "Gotta bounce—can't be late to fifth again. See ya, Ash."

I watch my one good friend in this whole crummy town disappear out the door.

Gentry doesn't exactly fit in with the normies around here. For starters, he's not shallow, the way most of those guys are. But that's not what makes him different. It's his vibe. His whole "rando couture" thing, as he calls it, started when his mom died and his dad would send him to school in whatever was clean, or at least not horribly dirty, no matter how mismatched or weird it was. Even in second grade, kids dragged him for it—I know because he came up to me one day, not long after I moved to Chico. He'd seen Wiz and them giving me a hard time about looking like a boy and came over. "Don't pay any attention to those guys," he said, throwing massive shade at them across the playground. "They make fun of everyone for everything. They've been doing it to me since second grade because . . ." He lifted the sides of his neon track jacket that he later confessed had been his mom's. "Those jerks called me a weirdo so many times, I just ran with it and made it my brand."

But underneath all that weird, Gentry's just a regular dude.

The thing is, I look like I'm trying to be a regular dude, too, and that's the problem.

It's hard enough for a guy who doesn't look like all the other guys in school.

It's even harder for a girl like me who does.

There Are 25,200 Seconds...

...in an average school day. Joss Cruz and I spend 10,800 of those seconds together. She's probably the most interesting person at Chico Junior, and three of our six classes are exactly the same subjects with exactly the same teachers. Half the day, not counting lunch. Considering I didn't even know her this time last week, these are pretty unlikely statistics, and yet they're true. What are the mathematical odds of *that* happening?

It doesn't feel unlucky to be around someone as rad as Joss Cruz three out of six classes every day. But some days, it doesn't exactly feel lucky either.

I curve my arm across the top of my desk in fifth period so no one can see what I'm drawing. Just when I make it to the fourth of eight undercover Joss panels, my name comes whooshing toward me like someone shot it out of a crossbow.

My head whips up.

"You're Ashley, correct?" the teacher says.

Mrs. Duncan should know my name by now, shouldn't she? We've been in school almost a whole week.

"Just Ash," I say.

"Well, Just Ash," Mrs. Duncan says. She's smiling, but I can't decide if it's a good smile or a not-good smile. "I see you're already hard at work, and I haven't even finished taking roll yet."

My face combusts.

I close my sketchbook so no one can see it, while the rest of the class giggles at her joke.

When she turns back to finish the roll, I pull my backpack into my lap and shove the sketchbook inside. Then I guard it with my life till the bell rings.

Joss sits somewhere behind me. I can't see her, but I know that if she wants to, she can see me. She can also *not* see me.

I bet Joss chooses to not see me.

Mrs. Duncan tells us to get out our Chromebooks.

She says, "We're going to be working on basic algebra concepts. Just to get our feet wet."

Whenever a teacher uses the word *basic*, you know a snoozefest is coming.

Only one more period to go and then I can get out of here.

Except then I have to go home.

Two Words...

PE.

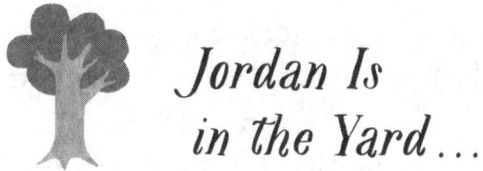
Jordan Is in the Yard...

...chopping wood when I get home from school. He must be mad or something. Ever since him and Renée moved in with us this summer, I've never seen Jordan do anything that counts as work.

Drago's metal iris closes around him as I walk down the gravel driveway. She would never let Jordan into her lair.

Today would be the perfect day to climb my favorite tree in the yard and draw, or think, or just listen to the world. There's a bunch of walnut trees around our rental, but only one is my favorite. Its branches start lower on the trunk, which makes it easier to climb, and also easier to hide in. The landlord warned us when we moved in that some of the trees were dying. I don't know how to tell if a tree is dying, but mine isn't. I'm sure of it.

I also know that, with Jordan making a bunch of

noise a few feet away, it won't be very relaxing to stay outside, even though I really want to.

I should be thinking about which tree the wood Jordan is chopping came from, but I'm not. All I'm thinking about is *my* tree, and how, thanks to Jordan, I can't hang out up there right now. When he first moved in with us, Gladys said, "Just think of Jordy like an uncle," but I can't. I can't think of any of them like they're family. It was better at Gladys's before Jordan and Renée moved in. She was less distracted, probably because there wasn't a baby to take care of. Besides, they aren't even supposed to live here, mostly because of Jordan's DUI. I heard Renée say something about it one night when they were fighting. But Gladys keeps saying it's only temporary, that soon Jordan and Renée and the baby will move into their own place. So far that hasn't happened. The only time they "move out" is every month or so when my caseworker is about to make a visitation.

"Hey," I say as I walk up to the house.

"Hey," he mumbles, barely looking at me. "How was school?"

Why do adults always ask that? It's obvious he doesn't really care about my answer, plus I never know what to say. I mean, it's school. I don't hate learning, but I don't like school that much. Actually, school would be okay if it wasn't full of people. So I guess the truth is, I mostly don't like people.

"It was whatevs," I say.

I catch the look he flicks in my direction.

"Whatevs, huh? What subject is that, exactly?" he asks, and I can't figure out why he cares so much about school, since he left school after tenth grade to go make his fortune on some crabbing boat in Alaska. Only that didn't happen, did it? Because why else would he have ended up back here?

I shrug him off and go inside.

Jordan's girlfriend isn't home. She works six days a week at the Grocery Outlet. "Someone's got to put food on the table," Renée says whenever she's leaving for her shift and Jordan's out of earshot. "Sure isn't gonna be him."

I sit at the kitchen table with a half-empty can of Thrifty Cola and some stale pretzels on a torn sheet of paper towel. Renée gets to bring home almost-expired food from the store sometimes, and even though Gladys is always supposed to have snacks in the house for me, stuff like stale pretzels is all Jordan lets me eat after school. Probably because he wants to keep the good snacks for himself.

I always thought Renée and Jordan were married until I heard him tell a girl at the corner market one time that they weren't. Only he said it ugly.

"I thought you had a wife," that girl said after Jordan leaned in and whispered something to her up at the cash register.

"Nah," he'd told her. "She's just my baby mama."

No one ever said you had to be married to have a baby. I mean, my mom wasn't married when she had me—she barely even knew my father. But I wonder if little Marcus coming along last year made Renée decide not to leave Jordan after all. Because before they came to live with us, Gladys would constantly say how Renée was fixing to leave him.

"Can't say I'd blame her, neither," she'd huff.

I take a few sips, then put the soda can back in the fridge for later.

Gladys comes out of the bedroom I *temporarily* share with Marcus. She says I can call her Grammy if I want, like some of her other foster kids did.

I don't.

"Finally got him down for a nap," she grunts. "Li'l cuss is as stubborn as his daddy. Don't make any noise, Ashley, you hear me?"

I'll make all the noise I know how if she calls me that name again after I've asked her a billion times not to.

I take my sketchbook out of my backpack instead of my notebook for school. I know I'm supposed to start working on my family tree, but I don't even know if I want to do one. I'd rather finish the last four Joss panels I started in class earlier, before I was rudely interrupted by Mrs. Duncan.

I wish Gladys would have gotten Marcus down for a nap at the usual time when I was still in school. That way, I could go to my room and draw in private.

Nothing's private out in the kitchen.

Not even my own private thoughts.

That's why I staked out a tree for myself out in the yard. But now I can't go there, either, because of Jordan.

It's amazing how lonely it can feel in a house where you never get to be anything close to alone.

Have You Ever...

...tried to sleep with a ten-month-old in a Pack 'n Play right next to your bed, in a room so small, he can reach out his hand and touch you in the middle of the night?

That's not even the hardest part about nighttime in this house. It's the fact that everything feels different with them here. That's what's hard—knowing how nights go now that we all live together.

Renée gets home from work around nine.

Jordan's usually a few beers in.

He's playing video games, or watching some cringe show with Gladys on the other end of the couch from him.

She's knitting a blanket or a sweater or socks, or going outside so she can smoke one cigarette after another. Adults aren't supposed to smoke around their fosters—I know because my caseworker, Barbara, had to remind Gladys about it three times during one of her home visits. And there's not supposed to be beer unless it's locked up.

Around ten, Gladys kicks them out of the living room so she can go to bed on the couch. She needs plenty of sleep so she can take care of Marcus six days a week. She was a lot less tired when it was just the two of us. We had our nighttime routine, too, but it wasn't as complicated. She'd ask if my homework was finished, and if it was, we'd sit on the couch with the TV on, her knitting and me drawing. At nine or so, she'd tell me it was time for bed. And she'd sleep in *her* room, which is now Jordan and Renée's room, which is next to my room, which I now have to share with Marcus.

I'm just glad Marcus is a heavy sleeper.

But I'm a not-heavy sleeper.

And they're heavy fighters.

I've heard him hit her before, but I'm not sure who to tell about it. Not his mother. She'd just take his side. I know that because, even though this is her house, she lets him make most of the house rules. Besides, Gladys would get in big trouble if I told anyone the truth about how things are around here now.

The only good thing I can remember happening was once, right after Jordan and Renée moved in, I was looking through boxes of stuff he was unpacking, and I saw this thing, this little circular thing with buttons on it that said OFF, ON, and PLAY.

"What's this?" I asked.

Jordan said, "It's just trash." And then he said, "It's called a Discman."

"What does it do?" I asked.

He pulled it out of the box, and a pair of flimsy headphones, too, with ear pads the size of quarters.

"Put those on," he said, and I did, and he pushed one of the buttons.

A band called Metallica came weaving through those dinky headphones.

He said, "My old man gave it to me, before he . . ." And then his voice trailed off, like the memory he was sharing got lost somewhere. When I looked close at his face, it seemed different. Softer than usual. Like wherever he'd drifted to, it must've been better than here.

But that didn't last long, because he snapped out of it a second later and went, "You can have it, if you want." He sniffed a couple of times, then handed me a few other CDs. Aerosmith. Whitesnake. Some band called Slayer.

"Might need new batteries," he mumbled.

The headphones don't do much to block out the noise of Jordan and Renée when they're in their room fighting, or when they're in their room not-fighting.

But if I turn Metallica up loud enough, it does help some.

And at least Marcus is a heavy sleeper.

 # *The Only Class...*

...Gentry and I have together this year is Miss Moua's homeroom, even though he says they just call it first period. Last year when Gladys and I moved here from Oroville, he and I were in the same fifth-grade class at Citrus. The day he came over to make me feel better about Wiz and them teasing me is the day we became friends.

Gentry's fine with all the touchy-feely stuff Miss Moua does in homeroom. He doesn't see it as a threat to his manhood, like Wiz and them seem to. Miss Moua doesn't *make* you share your feelings, but she encourages it.

My caseworker does a lot of get-in-touch-with-your-emotions stuff too. Barbara's not a bad person, she just tries to get me to share about how things are going at Gladys's house. But it always feels like a trick. Like, if I tell her how it's really going, that'll just make everything worse, not better.

Personally, I'm not a huge fan of sharing my feelings with other people.

It's different somehow with Miss Moua. On the first day at Chico Junior, she asked each of us what we wanted to be called, and I decided then that I was going to like her. She gets bonus teacher points for never calling me anything but Ash.

We even get to pick where we want to sit, and as long as we don't talk too much, she'll let us stay there. Who does that? None of my other teachers, that's for sure.

Today Miss Moua mentions she has a baby.

"Boy or girl?" someone asks, while a couple of girls squeal about it.

"Boy," she says, and now there's a scattering of questions.

"How old is he?" "What's his name?" "Did you name him after your husband?"

"I don't have a husband," she says.

"Boyfriend?" someone else asks.

"Nope. No boyfriend."

Dead silence.

Seems like everyone in homeroom is going to be chewing on that little nugget for a while.

I hang back at the end of class. Gentry turns at the doorway, looking surprised when I'm not right behind him. I wave goodbye to him, and he half waves back.

I know he must be confused about why I'm staying after, because even *I'm* confused about why I'm staying after.

"What's up, Ash?" Miss Moua says, leaning back in her chair.

"Can I ask you something?"

"Of course." She clicks out of the computer screen to give me her full attention. I'm not used to people giving me their full attention unless I'm about to get in trouble for something.

"I . . . How old is your baby?"

"Ten months," she says.

"Oh." I hold my breath for a few seconds, because Gladys has made me swear never to talk about our "situation" when I'm not at home. But for some reason, I blurt, "There's a ten-month-old baby at my house too."

She smiles, makes a kind of *oh* sound. "*Oh*. Baby brother? Baby sister?"

"Just . . . baby."

Miss Moua nods like this makes sense to her, only how could it? It's not like I just told her something revealing about my actual family.

Like I said, Gladys and them don't count.

I wish I did have one, though. I wish I had a mom like Miss Moua, who would talk about me to her class and smile the way Miss Moua did when she told us about her baby. The last time I saw *my* mom, she wasn't smiling like that. She wasn't smiling at all. She was looking straight ahead as they handcuffed her and took her to jail while the firefighters sprayed water on our house from a giant hose. She didn't even wish me happy birthday.

Having your mom go to jail on your fourth birthday isn't a great present.

I don't know what to say next, so I go, "Okay, well. See you Monday."

She smiles. "See you Monday, Ash."

I walk toward second period without paying attention.

I'm thinking about Miss Moua.

I'm thinking about how she has a baby but doesn't have a husband or a boyfriend.

I'm thinking about how her baby is ten months old, just like Marcus.

I'm thinking about how weird it is to have something in common with my teacher. Even something minuscule like that.

I am not thinking about science, or Mr. Torres, or Wiz Porter.

But I should be.

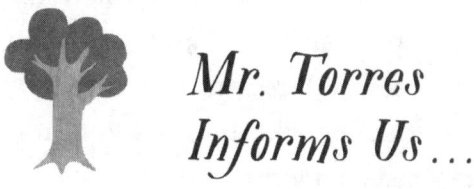
Mr. Torres Informs Us...

...**that we will start the** year by studying matter. Its physical properties. Its chemical properties. Its different states.

"Matter matters," he says.

No one laughs, but one girl calls out, "Dad jokes are bad jokes," and that's actually kind of funny.

It's bad enough Mr. Torres wants us to work with a partner.

But then he says, "It's not that I don't trust you to put yourselves into pairs, I just don't trust you not to match up with your besties. So I've gone ahead and done it for you." He acts like he's doing us a huge favor by choosing our partners so we don't have to.

He is not doing *me* a favor by matching me with Wiz Porter. But Wiz smiles at me like he thinks he's doing me a favor by "letting" me be his science partner.

"Guaranteed A," he says, sliding in next to me when Mr. Torres has us change seats. "I'm a wizard."

"No, you're not."

Wiz stinks like he dumped a whole can of Axe body spray on himself before leaving for school this morning, which is better than his usual stink. I know that specific smell because I get the same whiff off Jordan sometimes, even though he swears to Gladys he doesn't smoke weed anymore.

When Mr. Torres asks, "Does anyone need to make any adjustments before we get started?" I raise my hand.

He consults his seating chart before saying, "Ashley?"

I try not to grind my teeth too hard when I say, "It's just Ash," since I'm about to ask him to do me a solid. "Can I move? My partner smells like an entire can of Axe."

Wiz looks at me with disgust and goes, "Well, you smell like sweaty feet."

"And he thinks he's a wizard."

Mr. Torres hits me with one of those plutonium-grade teacher looks.

He says, "I meant I would consider adjustments for things like vision. Or hearing."

I squint at Mr. Torres.

"I can't see or hear from where I'm sitting," I say.

Mr. Torres checks his computer screen real quick, and for a second or two I think he may actually move me.

But then he just looks up again and says, "Anyone

have an *actual* issue?" And without leaving time to answer, he goes, "Good. Let's get to it."

Wiz practically tears open the zipper on his backpack like a hyena ripping the flesh off an antelope. The sound is so jarring, I swing around fast—so fast, he doesn't have time to hide the baggie of joints inside. Three of them, just sitting there all casual, like a Ziploc full of Cheetos his mom packed him for a snack.

I look up in surprise, and he looks back at me, frozen with something like shock, or fear.

I want to ask him if they're real, but they must be. I smell it on him all the time.

He grabs a pencil from inside, then zips his bag closed as quick as he opened it and slings another worried glance at me as Mr. Torres starts talking about the properties of matter.

I'm not going to snitch, if that's what Wiz is thinking.

Maybe I should. But I have my own secrets, and I sure wouldn't want someone to spill mine to the whole world.

Things Don't Get Better...

...in English.

Ms. Kim starts the period with a free write. Only it's not a free write. She wants us to finish the sentence:

What I wish Ms. Kim knew about me...

I don't wish Ms. Kim knew anything about me.

I flip to my sketchbook, hidden at the back of my notebook, and draw Ms. Kim as a three-headed supervillain.

I'm concentrating so hard on the details of her three villain faces, I have no idea that the real Ms. Kim is standing behind me until her voice bounces off the top of my head and splats onto the page.

"See me after class, Ash," she says soft and low from right next to me.

When the bell rings, I wait till everyone else is gone, then shuffle up to her desk.

"Sit down," she says. "Finish your free write."

"I'll be late for social studies."

"I'll write you a pass."

I stare at my paper.

What I wish Ms. Kim knew about me . . .

I put, *I never learned how to write—I only know how to draw. From now on, I'll be drawing all my assignments. Thank you for understanding.*

I hand it to her, and she reads it. She reaches into her drawer, writes something on a small piece of paper, gives it to me.

"*Detention?*" I ask. "Why am I getting detention?"

"It's not detention," she says. "It's a note saying to come back after school on Monday so you can finish this. Maybe give your answer some extra thought over the weekend. Consider it a reminder to make whatever arrangements you need so you can stay after school."

"You didn't even read me my *Miranda* rights," I mumble, taking the paper.

She smiles like she thinks I'm being funny.

"Have a good weekend, Ash," she says.

I wonder how I'm going to tell Gladys I need to stay late on Monday. Or if she's going to snitch to Jordan about it, since he fakes being so interested in what I do at school.

Maybe I'll wait till Sunday night to mention it. Now that Jordan lives with us, he almost always takes over the discipline stuff. Like he thinks he's the dad or something.

Which is a joke, because he barely wants to be a dad to his own actual kid.

Our Family Tree Assignment...

...is due next Thursday.

Mr. Mann reminds us of this on Friday, only he says *dynasty assignment* instead.

One week isn't enough time to come up with a family tree. But it's also too much time. It's actually a pretty long time to have to think about a family tree with nothing on it but a mom who got sent to jail on your fourth birthday, and a bunch of foster families that Mr. Mann would probably say don't count. Not even the Silvas, and they were my almost-real family for a while. Almost-real families do things like teach you how to finally tie your shoes in third grade, when all the other kids knew how by first. They help you with your homework after school, and make sure you brush *and* floss your teeth at night, and tell you you're a great kid after someone hurts your feelings. They don't stop reading you bedtime stories just because you're eight years old, and they don't make you feel bad about how much you like it. That's what made Joe and Ana Silva my almost-real family.

Almost-real families are like real families, only you don't know if they're forever or not.

Wiz Porter and Chase Williams crowd around Steven Tyler's desk while we're supposed to be working on our assignment in class. I don't know why Wiz hangs out with them—they treat him like he's a disease. But he lets them do it, just so he can be part of their group, I guess.

Right now, they keep bumping into Joss's desk. I'm not watching, but I hear her say "Quit bumping my desk!" more than once.

"It's because, look," Steven Tyler says, flipping his phone around to show her.

I can't see what's on it.

But Joss can.

"You guys are jerks," she says.

Whatever they're looking at, Gentry will probably see it and tell me about it at lunch, since I can't get internet or even pictures with the cheap gas station Tracfone Gladys bought me.

I'm not working on my family tree either. I'm drawing Wiz and them in quicksand, with their arms over their heads. They're yelling for help. Quicksand's a good thing to draw guys like Chase and Wiz and Steven Tyler in, because it never happens in places like Chico. If anyone saw the drawing, they couldn't say I was threatening to drown those guys in quicksand.

Something's not a threat if there's no realistic chance of you doing it to them.

"Hey."

The word comes at me short and sharp, like a dart. I almost don't want to look up in case whoever said it has stuck an invisible bull's-eye on my forehead.

Joss drops into my eyeline.

"Can you show me how to draw an old man?" she says kinda loud, throwing a look toward Wiz and them.

"I . . . *What*?"

"You draw pretty good," she says, being all weird about it. "Show me how to draw an old man."

She sits down on the seat next to mine and scooches in close. Usually Leti Moreno sits there, but Leti is currently on top of Taryn Swisher's desk on the other side of me. They don't look like they're working on their projects, either, but they might be. It's hard to tell—there's a lot going on in the room right now.

Joss leans in and whispers, "You might not want to go to the cafeteria at lunch."

I blink up at her. Just because she's cool and sounds smart doesn't mean she can be trusted. I don't know Joss Cruz any more than I know anyone else in this stupid school, other than Gentry—most of us literally just met five days ago. But so far there's no evidence that she's actually trustworthy.

"They're planning something," she adds.

Trying to find the truth in her eyes feels like going on a scavenger hunt.

"Planning what?" I ask.

"I don't know, but . . ." She sneaks a peek over her shoulder at Wiz and them, still clustered together around Steven Tyler's phone, before turning back to me.

"It doesn't sound good," she adds, trying to look over my arm at my sketchbook. I slowly close the cover so she can't see what I'm drawing.

"Do you really want to learn how to draw an old man?" I ask, staring right at her.

Her light-brown eyes stare right back without blinking. "No."

I throw a quick stealth look at the guys. "Why would you come over here to secretly tell me that?" I ask. "About them?"

"Because they're jerks, and they always get away with it."

I want to believe her. But I don't know how to believe people I don't know very well.

The problem is, I don't usually get a chance to know *anyone* very well.

Nine foster families in almost eight years makes it hard. It's not enough time to know if you can trust people. It's definitely not long enough to believe in them. Except for the Silvas. I was with them for a year and a half. Long enough for them to want to adopt me, before everything went wrong. "We always planned to have a boy and a girl—our dream family," Ana Silva had said once. She was crying, so I put my arm around her and imagined her sadness like it was a plushie I could hold for her until she needed it back. Then she wiped her tears and straightened up and said, "But I think God meant for us to be your parents," and I was happy, because it felt like that was true. Until the day they called me into the kitchen and she said, "I have some . . . surprising news. I'm having twins. A boy and a girl." I smiled so big and said, "I'm going to be a big sister?" And the look on their faces. On hers when she said, "I'm so sorry, sweetheart. I always thought you'd stay with us." On his when he said, "We'd keep you if we could, but money's just gonna be so tight now . . ."

I was with them long enough for me to believe in them, and that got me exactly nowhere.

So I guess that's what I am . . .

A kid with no one to believe in.

 # *Since Mr. Mann...*

...isn't paying attention anyway, I pull my phone out near the end of class and message Gentry under the desk to meet me by the library instead of the cafeteria. Joss might be trying to trick me, but why take any unnecessary chances?

"I was just about to text," Gentry says when I walk up to him outside the library. "I heard those guys talking about you, but I only heard your name, not what they were saying."

That does fit with what Joss told me.

"Wanna know what they did this time?" he asks.

"Uh . . . I dunno. Do I?"

He pulls up their latest Photoshop.

They've taken the liberty of making my family tree for me.

It's supposed to be a joke, but it's not funny. A chart full of drag queens and hypermasculine female athletes and people screen-grabbed from Pride pictures isn't funny. It's mean.

I can tell Gentry feels bad about it, so I say, "Well,

that's just a disappointing effort. Complete amateur hour."

He doesn't laugh. He asks, "What's it supposed to be?" as I take his phone from him.

"My family tree." I open up his photo app and add the words *Lacking in Creativity* across the front, with the letter *F* in a red circle. When I'm done, I look up and say, "It's that stupid assignment for Mann's class."

"We don't have to do anything like that for Noe's."

I wonder if they'd let me move to Mr. Noe's class. Usually, you have to have a compelling reason to switch out.

Family tree assignments aren't a compelling reason to switch out. Axe body spray is not a compelling reason to switch out. Bullying could be, but no one would use that excuse, because it would make you a snitch if you did.

"So, if we can't go to the caf," Gentry asks, squinting down the hall in that direction, "where can we go?"

I spot Joss coming down the main hallway. She cuts a hard left and heads straight for the cafeteria.

"You know what?" I say. "Let's just go."

His face turns paler than it usually is. "But I thought you said—?"

"I got bad intel."

Gentry's not a scaredy-cat, but there's a difference

between being a scaredy-cat and being scared. He looks scared.

"Come on," I say, pulling him by the backpack strap for a few steps. "I'll share my nachos with you."

He yanks out of my grip. "You're going to the cafeteria, *and* you're getting food?"

"Yup."

"Because . . . you have a death wish?"

"No." I lock eyes with his. The indigo blue of them looking almost black right now. "Because I'm hungry."

I push my long bangs away from my eyes and hold his stare, but he doesn't move, not even when I hike the straps of my backpack higher on my shoulders like someone prepping for battle.

He's not the only one who's nervous. I'm nervous too.

But I'm also mad. I'm mad at those guys and the offensive family tree they made, like they think someone like me must come from an all-gay circus family. I'm mad at Joss for telling me something bad was going to happen if I went to the cafeteria today, when *she* can waltz right in there because nothing bad would ever happen to her. I'm mad that I had to move to this town, just because Jordan knocked up his fake wife after a fight one night, and Gladys got a bigger house so they could fake–move in with us. I'm mad that all Gladys worries about now is taking care of Marcus, when she used to be focused on taking care of me—especially because now Jordan acts like he's team leader. And I'm mad that the new, *bigger* house isn't even big enough for me to have my own room, or any kind of privacy at all.

And that's all there is to know about my so-called family.

1 Gentry Follows Me...

... to the food line where I pick up a tray and load it with nachos and apple slices and milk. I swipe my lunch card, and the lady in the hairnet tells me to have a good day.

That's the easy part.

The harder part is finding a place to sit that isn't near Wiz and them, but also isn't right up next to the lunchroom monitor. Otherwise, we'd look like a couple of losers who need a teacher with a whistle for protection.

There's a table near the water bottle filling station with room at one end. We sit there so we can keep an eye on Wiz and them, even though they don't seem to notice we're here. I scan the cafeteria for Joss, find her all the way down at the other end of the room. She's laughing with her friends, just like yesterday.

So far, no one's rushing over to knock my lunch tray in the air. No one's kicking their foot out as I pass by and laughing as my food goes sailing. Besides, we have a one-eighty view of our surroundings. Wiz and

Chase and Steven Tyler are in our eyeline, and they're not even paying attention to us. I can see Joss, too, if I want. Sometimes I do want to see Joss. But not now. Now definitely isn't one of those times.

All I want to do now is bask in the glory of sinking my teeth into some crunchy, gooey nachos right here in the cafeteria, with the added bonus of knowing where my enemies are.

Which is why it's so shocking when Matt Adams slides in beside me on the seat bench. I shoot a look across the room and realize too late—he wasn't with Wiz and them when we got here. It's usually all four, but idiot me didn't do a head count.

"So, is it *Ash*?" he asks into the side of my face. "Or *Ashley*? Which is it?"

My heart goes into hyperdrive. I notice the way Gentry swallows, and not because he's eating. I never even got a chance to open the chip packet.

"Who's your boyfriend, *Ashley*?" Matt says, fluffing up the ruffles along the front of Gentry's tuxedo shirt. "That's who this little freak is, right? Your *boyfriend*? I mean . . . you're always together, so."

I want to tell Gentry to leave so he doesn't have to be sucked into this, but I can't say it without Matt hearing. Besides, Wiz and them must have seen Matt come over, and now we're completely boxed in by a four-pack of jerks.

Gentry starts pulling at the satin bow tie around his neck, like it's choking him.

"Look, guys," Matt says. "*Ashley* bought us lunch."

"How are the nachos, *Ashley*?" Steven Tyler says. "Here. Lemme try 'em for ya. I'll give you my honest review."

He opens the nacho cheese packet with his teeth, squeezes some of the cheese sauce into his mouth. He passes it to Wiz, and then Chase grabs it from him, wraps his nasty lips around the opening, and sucks the cheese sauce until it's almost empty.

Wiz takes the apple slices. "So kind of you to buy us lunch, *Ashley*," he says. "It's the least you could do, since we made your family tree project for you."

"No need to thank us, *Ashley*," Matt says, nastiness dripping off every word. "It was our pleasure." He smashes the chips in the chip packet to smithereens.

"You know what?" Steven Tyler says, a glob of nacho sauce plopping onto his Aerosmith shirt from his chin. "Where are our manners? These two lovebirds were trying to have a romantic lunch, and we just crashed right into the middle of it."

"Maybe they should kiss," Wiz says, leaning in close. He stinks like pot and Axe.

"Yeah." Steven Tyler makes a nasty face. "*Kiss*. And we'll leave you alone."

"Kiss," Matt chimes in, and with the four of them surrounding us, their chants of "Kiss, kiss, kiss, kiss!" pick up steam.

The lunchroom teacher finally notices and blows her whistle as she heads over.

The four of them crack apart, Matt still making kissing noises and Steven Tyler warning "To be continued" as they stand up to leave.

I don't move.

I can't.

After a beat, Gentry asks, "You okay?"

I keep my head down as I nod.

With Wiz and them leaving the cafeteria, the teacher with the whistle goes back to her spot up against the stage. Chatter and laughter drift back into the air that had gone empty a minute before.

Gentry goes, "Hey, Ash?" and I look up.

"I woulda done it," he says real soft.

My face scrunches up. "Done *what*?"

"I woulda kissed you, if it meant saving our lives."

I want to cry, because what just happened with those guys was humiliating. But I also don't want to cry, because I think what Gentry offered afterward makes him the best friend I've ever had. Like a brother. Sometimes I think about how I could have had a brother *and* a sister if the Silvas would have let me stay. But I've never come even close to having a best friend before Gentry.

"Dude." He taps me on the leg, and I brace against whatever's coming next. But he doesn't say anything else, just tips his chin a few times.

I follow his gaze.

Joss is on the other side of the cafeteria, still sitting at her table even though her friends are gone already.

She stares at me in some kind of confusing way. Man, I can't figure her out. Not that look on her face. Or the way she acts—how she's cool one minute and cold the next.

I don't know what to do with the way she's looking at me, so I just swing my back to her, get up, and follow Gentry out of the cafeteria.

Joss Tries to Talk to Me...

... in math class.

I keep my eyes on the smartboard so I don't get in trouble. Girls like her don't usually get in trouble for talking in class, but girls like me always do.

Principles of Algebra. I scribble the words on my paper, then add in a bunch of algebra-looking symbols that I may or may not have invented myself. Mrs. Duncan starts writing real equations on the board and tells us to copy them onto our paper.

Somehow, Joss gets Eddie Hinojosa to switch seats with her behind Mrs. Duncan's back.

"I'm sorry about what those guys did," she whispers.

$5x + 3 = 7x - 1$

"I tried to warn you," she whispers, a shade louder this time.

$5(z + 1) = 3(z + 2) + 11$

"Ash . . . ," she whispers.

I squinch my eyes and shout, "*Shut up!*"

Everyone in the room spins in our direction, including Mrs. Duncan.

My hand shoots into the air.

"Can I have a pass to the restroom?" I blurt without waiting to be called on.

"Boys' or girls'?" some dude in the back mumbles. A few people laugh.

Mrs. Duncan has that teacher look of disapproval, but she motions to a wooden "potty pass" hanging near the door.

It's probably not a good idea to give someone who's already mad a big wooden stick for a hall pass, but I grab my backpack and leave class with it anyway.

I'm not even halfway down the hall when Joss comes rocketing in my direction.

"Ash! Wait a sec!"

She catches up to me, although there's a slight chance I may have slowed down a little and let her.

I go, "How'd you even get out? I'm the one with the"—I wave the stick—"lethal weapon."

"I asked Mrs. Duncan if I could come check on you."

I squint at her. "How come?"

"Because . . . I feel bad about what happened. Those guys are jerks, and . . . I tried to tell you."

"It's not about what happened. I mean, it is. It sucked, and it made me mad. But . . . it's not . . ."

Joss's face spins through a bunch of different expressions, until it finally lands on confused.

"Then, *what*?"

"I mean . . . if you *knew* something bad was going to happen, why would you just sit there and let it? Like yesterday . . . when Matt showed you that picture on his phone, that Photoshop—"

"I know which picture," she says.

I lean back.

Joss stands there. Staring. Waiting.

"You laughed," I say. "You laughed at a nasty picture that was supposed to be me."

She shakes her head, and her hair spirals around her shoulders.

"I didn't laugh at that picture, Ash."

"Yes, you did."

I shove my hands into my pockets. The note Ms. Kim gave me crinkles against my knuckles, reminding me what a bad day this has already been. And then lunch happened, and now—

Joss is still shaking her head.

"You did too," I say. "I *heard* you. And then, today? You just sat there while those guys were messing with me and Gentry, and you didn't even come over and try to stop it."

She throws all her weight to one side, looks around, looks at me.

"A girl shouldn't do that to another girl," I say.

She doesn't look away. Maybe she wants to. But she doesn't.

"I don't . . . I don't think of you as . . ."

The skin under my hair tingles. "As *what*? A girl?"

"*No.*" She licks her lips. "You come off like a . . . like this really strong person. Like whatever happens, you just . . . handle it."

She's right. I do handle it. I *handle it* when Jordan can't control his anger. I *handle it* when Gladys thinks I'm asleep and I can hear her call me ugly names out in the living room, even with my Discman on. Or she leaves Marcus in his crib for so long, I end up having to feed him and change his diaper. Or when Jordan rages at Renée after she's worked all day for six days in a row. Or when kids at school make disgusting Photoshop pictures of me. I do handle it. But I shouldn't have to.

I tell Joss, "Yeah, well . . . just because I'm handling it? Doesn't mean you should sit there and watch me."

Since I'm the one who's always in trouble anyway, I hand her Mrs. Duncan's potty pass so *she* doesn't get in trouble on her way back to class. Then I dip into the bathroom to wash this bad day off my face.

And Then There's the Travesty...

... of PE.

Because now that we're officially in middle school, we have to wear gym clothes for PE.

Last year in fifth grade, we could play sports in our regular clothes. And we only had PE a couple of times a week. This year, we have it every day, and every day we have to change out.

Starting today.

There's a long rack of shirts and shorts right on top of the painted C in the middle of the gym floor. Everything's separated by size. That's the first crummy thing about having to change for PE. Some people feel shy about what size they wear, but too bad for them, I guess, because they make us pick our size right in front of everyone.

Then we have to take our shirt and shorts into the girls' locker room and change.

In front of everyone.

They give us a lock with a combination. They tell us to remember the combination. They tell us not to lose the paper with the combination on it or share that number with anyone, not even our friends. They tell us for now to stick the paper inside our shoe or sock until we for sure have it memorized.

And then they tell us to meet in the gym in five minutes.

Wearing our new PE clothes.

I keep my eyes glued to the slip of paper with my locker number and combination on it as I go into the girls' locker room, so no one can say I was looking at them while they were getting undressed.

I whisper in an unhearable voice while I look for my locker. "Please let it be in the back. Please let it be in the back."

It's not in the back.

It's right in the middle of everyone.

In between each row of lockers there's a row of low benches. I sit facing my locker, holding the new PE clothes I'm supposed to switch into, staring at the piece of paper with my combination on it.

I sit.

And wait.

Until all the other girls are dressed and gone.

Then I change into my PE clothes.

When I get out to the gym, I'm late.

Coach Miller tells me to go sit on the bleachers until she can talk to me.

I know what that means.

It means I'm now in double trouble on the first Friday of middle school.

It means she might call Gladys.

It means Gladys will probably tell Jordan about it, and Jordan will say something like, *Funny how other people always act up and you always get in trouble for it, ain't it, Ash?* And I'll have to stay in my room all weekend and watch Marcus as a punishment.

Which isn't that different from most weekends, I guess. Except that everyone will be extra mad at me. Madder than usual.

Coach Miller finishes her pep talk to the class and sends them off to run laps. Then she comes over to the bleachers and sits next to me.

She doesn't say anything right away, which feels like a trick. I'm not going to be the first one to speak up, that's for sure, since that's probably what she wants me to do.

Coach Miller lets out a sigh.

"The first few weeks of middle school can be rough."

Another trick. She'll start out nice, then *wa-POW*. You're in detention till the end of the year. I know how these things go.

"Lots of changes," Coach says. "New people. New ways of doing things. It's all just a lot to get used to."

I don't say anything. Don't even look at her. Just stick my hand out, palm up as the *thud-thud-thud* of gym shoes rumbles past us.

"What's that for?" she asks.

"Can we just skip to the part where you give me detention?" I say.

She does one of those soft-laugh-through-her-nose things. In my side vision, I notice her leaning back on her elbows.

"Two more laps!" she calls out to the class. Some of the kids groan.

I'm still holding out my hand.

"For what it's worth," she says, "I don't believe in giving detention."

My hand slowly reels itself back in.

"Why not?" I'm still skep, still expecting the angry-teacher version of Coach Miller to flip on me any second.

She goes, "I don't think it lends anything positive to the situation."

For a minute, all I hear is the squeak of tennis shoes rounding the corner.

"So, what's my punishment?" I ask.

"For what?"

"For being late to class?"

She pushes off her elbows, leans forward so she can see me better.

Instead of answering me, she asks, "How do you feel right now?"

I finally look at her. I look and look and don't stop.

"I don't like to tell people how I feel."

"Why not?"

Because, I think. No one wants to know how you feel if it's going to make them sad. Like that time I came down the slide too fast in kindergarten and landed in a puddle, and everyone laughed and said I'd peed my pants. The yard-duty teacher pulled me aside and asked, "Want me to call your mommy and see if she can bring you a new pair?" And I told her, "My mom can't come. She's in jail." And that look on her face. Like I'd just ruined her whole birthday party or something.

I tell Coach Miller, "People just use your feelings against you."

She nods like she gets it, but I bet she doesn't. Anyone can nod like that and not get it.

"Why don't you take the last lap with the class?" she finally says.

I get up.

Look back at Coach Miller.

Wait for her to yell at me to sit back down.

Watch for some alien monster to bust out through her chest.

Or send me to the principal's office for defiance or something.

But she just nods toward the other students as they run under the basketball hoop at the end of the gym.

I'm still confused as I skip down the bleachers and join them for the last lap.

Gym class can't be this easy. I've heard too many stories, seen too many TV shows.

One of these days, I know the sky is gonna fall.

I Spend a While in My Tree...

...when I first get home from school. It's already been a bad-enough day—I just need to breathe easy for a few minutes before going inside to whatever today's flavor of drama is.

Once I find a high-enough branch, I close my eyes. Run my fingers across the jaggy limb I'm perched on. Think about how trees are like people sometimes. Rough on the outside, but then the inside, like tree rings, can tell a whole different story. That's what I hoped Jordan would be like at first—that he was just rough on the outside. Because it seemed like maybe there were other layers to him. He even said he'd build me a tree house. "Right here in this tree," he told me. "Gladys says it's your favorite." But he never even mentioned it again once he lived here. And I've never seen anything that seems like a story he carries inside him either. Almost like he's all bark and no rings.

When I realize there's no noise coming from the house, my Drago senses go off. I lean forward and strain to listen. No talking, or yelling, or arguing. The baby isn't even crying. I don't know what it means, only that it seems like the perfect time to go inside. I just need to stay low-key, see if I can keep off their radar tonight.

I head straight for my room. No snacks. No TV. No nothing.

"Why don't you take Marcus in there with you?" Gladys calls out as I walk by. "I'm exhausted. That rash of his is keeping us both up. He ain't even napping these days, he screams so bad."

I know all about that—I sleep right next to him. She's not the only one who needs a break from his crying.

"I have homework," I say, shutting the door behind me, loud enough to be heard but not hard enough to be a slam. Jordan hates when anyone slams doors.

But that doesn't stop him from barging into my room two seconds later, a longneck in his fist, stinking like maybe it's not his first beer of the day.

"Did Gladys ask you to watch Marcus?" he says. I know it's not a question, even though it sounds like one.

I start pulling stuff out of my backpack.

"Isn't that the whole reason you guys are here? So she can watch Marcus?" I say. Two people can play the it-sounds-like-a-question-but-it's-not-really-a-question game.

"If that woman asks you to do something, you do it. Understood?"

I plop my binder on top of my books on top of the bed and look up at him.

"How am I supposed to do my homework when he's in here?"

"Just leave him in the crib," he says, waving his hand impatiently in the direction of Marcus's Pack 'n Play. A Pack 'n Play isn't a crib—even I know that, and I'm never going to have kids. Gladys told Jordan to just get something they could fold up fast and take somewhere else once every month or two when my caseworker comes for a home visit. She said that way, it wouldn't look like they lived here.

"Why don't *you* watch him?" I mumble.

Jordan is almost out the door, but he stops and turns, which means he heard me.

He goes, "Excuse me?" and I know I'm in it deep. But I can't stop myself.

"I said, why don't *you* watch him? He's your kid."

Jordan has never hit me. He's only ever hit Renée, and Gladys's old dog Frampton, and he's swatted Marcus on the butt a few times. But he looks like he could hit me now. Like he really, really wants to.

"Don't you ever back talk me," he says. "You hear?"

I blink at him, trying not to show fear. That's

usually when he hits Renée—when she looks like she's scared he might.

"*Don't you ever back talk me like that!*" he yells, slapping the wall.

I jump from the sound, even though I swore myself not to.

After he leaves my room, I don't move a muscle. I know better when he's on a rant, and his angry voice is out there, still bouncing all over the whole house.

And I still haven't moved when he comes back with Marcus.

He shoves the baby at me.

"I don't care *what* you do with him," he spits. "I don't want to see either of you the rest of the day."

He slams out the door, and I look at Marcus, and Marcus looks at me. I don't want to touch his rashy little butt or his snotty little nose, but I know that sooner or later I'll have to.

One thing's for sure—I'm not making him stay in a rickety Pack 'n Play all day and night. That's not fair. He's just a baby. He didn't do anything bad.

I'm the one who's always bad.

With my free hand, I fish some old broken crayons out of a drawer and tear a few sheets of binder paper out of my notebook so Marcus has something to do while I draw. He babbles as he makes random marks on the paper with a green crayon.

In my sketchbook, I draw a picture of Drago buying groceries from Renée, who's standing at the cash register of the Grocery Outlet. They're strategizing ways to take Jordan down—Drago wants to help her with that. Renée usually has her hair up when she goes to work—her messy bun. Sometimes, when she gets home, I notice how it's even messier than when she left. How some of her hair is hanging loose around her face. I used to wear mine long when I was little, but it didn't look pretty on me like it does on her. I didn't really want long hair, but my mom loved brushing it out and putting it in cute styles. I just think, with as thin and straight as my hair is, it looks better when it's short. Renée's is kind of curly and full. Lucky for me, she knows how to cut hair pretty well, so I let her do mine. She does it how I like—short on one side, a little longer on the other, so the bangs can fall like curtains over my eyes if I want them to. Jordan makes fun of her, saying it's the only hairstyle she knows how to do.

And he makes fun of me for having *boy hair*. That's what he calls it.

As if only boys can wear their hair short like this.

As if looking more like his idea of a boy than his idea of a girl is the worst way you can be.

It Looks Like Jordan's Plans for the Weekend...

...**involve bingeing on beer** and *Call of Duty*.

The one good thing about him game bingeing is that he pretty much ignores the rest of us. He's physically attached to the old Xbox he traded his tools for a while back. Said he didn't need the tools anymore once he "got hurt" on the job. He's not *that* hurt—just enough not to do stuff he doesn't want to do, like his old construction job, or house chores, or watching Marcus. But he can still shoot hoops with his buddies. Or go four-wheeling whenever his friend Kenny invites him.

Or chop wood, apparently.

When Gladys says she's taking Marcus downtown on Saturday, I don't ask her what she's doing, only if I can have a ride.

"I'm supposed to meet Gentry for a study session," I tell her, since he's the only friend whose house I'm allowed to hang out at. Not that I've asked if I could go to anyone else's house. I mean, who else would I want to kick it with after school or on a Saturday? I don't have any real friends besides Gentry.

Anyway, it's a total waste of a lie. If Gladys cared about what I was doing, she would have asked me about it, but she didn't. She never does.

"You can drop me off at the skate park," I add. "Me and Gentry can walk to his house from there."

She doesn't correct my bad grammar the way the Silvas used to. They didn't do it to be mean. It was just a way of helping me, because I was a little behind in language arts when I went to live with them in third grade.

Hey, Ana! Me and Joe shot baskets on the playground when he picked me up from school.

That's awesome, Ash. Joe and I used to play basketball there all the time when we were dating. Maybe we can all go play one evening after dinner—would you like that?

When I heard her say it back like that, *Joe and I used to play*, I tucked it in my brain files for next time. I wanted to learn to talk like them so people would know we were a family.

But all Gladys says is "Sit in the back with the baby."

It's deathly quiet the whole way down the Esplanade, and as we turn onto Humboldt toward the skate park, she goes, "When are you gonna be done?"

"I don't know." I send out a quick text to see how far away Gentry is. "I'm sure I can get a ride home, though."

Gladys stops in front of the skate park at the same time Gentry and his dad, Sam, roll up on the other side of the street. Gentry pops out of the car, and I shake my head. He's dressed straight out of the '90s in head-to-toe neon. Man, he's such a weirdo.

He busts into a smile as I jog across Humboldt to meet him.

"Hey, Ash," Sam Noble says from the driver's seat of the car.

"Hey, Sam," I say back.

"How's life?"

"Um . . ."

"Can we have some money for Dutch Bros?" Gentry asks his dad.

"Why don't you just go to 7-Eleven? It's cheaper," Sam says. He doesn't get the appeal of Dutch Bros because his go-to drink is always cola Slurpees at 7-Eleven. But Slurpees don't come in awesome flavors like Unicorn Blood and Dragon Slayer, and besides . . . a Slurpee isn't an energy drink.

"It's not the same," Gentry tells him.

"Didn't I give you five dollars yesterday?" Sam asks.

Gentry goes, "Uh . . . yeah. But five bucks isn't enough for two drinks."

"It is at 7-Eleven," Sam says with a wink, pulling

his wallet out and handing him a Hamilton. "That's it until payday, bud," he adds. "Spend it wisely."

Gentry stuffs the bill into his pocket.

As we head toward Dutch Bros, he goes, "I take it you didn't tell Gladys you have to stay after school on Monday?"

"Nope. She'd probably just think it was detention and I'd be grounded right now."

"Yeah, but don't you have to ask her to pick you up late?"

"Not today, I don't."

He gives me a sly look. "Riiiiight. Cuz if you wait till Sunday night, she can't ground you for the weekend."

"Exactly."

"Good call." He fist-bumps me, lets his explode. His skinny fingers look more like jellyfish tentacles than the blast waves of an explosion.

We swing into Dutch Bros and wait for our turn to order, and when we're up, Gentry tells the girl at the window what we each want, because we always get the same thing every time. He pulls his money out and pays for both of us.

A few minutes later, we head back down the street to Humboldt Park with our drinks and sit on the low wall, watching the skaters and bladers and bikers do their thing.

"Don't look now," he says into his straw, "but—"

"My dudes!"

Joss Cruz appears out of nowhere, skateboard tucked under her arm, and sits down like we were chilling here just waiting for her.

She goes, "So, what are we talking about?"

"Quantum physics," Gentry says with a totally straight face.

She looks at me like she knows that can't be right.

"Yeah?" She tips her chin my way. "What's *your* favorite thing about quantum physics, Ash?"

"I'm a huge fan of quarks," I tell her, mostly because that's the only word I remember from an introductory science unit last year that the teacher was *way* too excited about. I swear, quantum physics was my fifth-grade teacher's kink.

Meanwhile, Joss just sits there, watching me like I'm supposed to go into some kind of explanation about it. Honestly, I don't know *what* to say to her—after the way we left off yesterday, I'm surprised she's even talking to me today.

Gentry looks back and forth between us, and for a few clicks, no one says anything. Long enough for things to get awkward.

"It was a joke," I add. "Quarks?"

"Yeah," she says. "I heard you."

But she doesn't laugh, so I'm not sure if my joke wasn't funny specifically, or if Joss just thinks *I'm* not funny in general.

"What are *you* doing here?" Gentry finally asks her.

"Skating, obviously."

Only she's watching *me* as I spin my straw around inside my cup.

"What flavor did you get?" she asks.

"Dragon Slayer."

She makes a face and turns to Gentry. "What about you?"

"Galaxy Fish."

"Oh! Can I have a sip? I don't have cooties or anything."

Did she say *cooties*? Like in grade school?

Joss leans in to take a hit off Gentry's drink and gets instant brain freeze. He laughs as her face squinches up and she smacks her hand against her forehead.

And because I can't let things go, I ask her, "What do you have against quarks?"

She giggles into the straw as she takes another sip. "You're a dork."

"Fine. What do you have against Dragon Slayer?"

"It turns your tongue blue," she says.

The cold inside my mouth turns to heat across my face.

"It does?"

"Stick your tongue out," Gentry says.

I don't want to stick my tongue out in front of them, but I now have to—they're both staring at me.

I look away, pop my tongue out real fast.

Those two burst into laughter at the same time.

"Man, that does it," I say. "I'm switching to Unicorn Blood."

That one's not even red, just a pale shade of orange.

Gentry points to Joss's deck and goes, "So, you really skate, or what?"

She shrugs. "Sometimes."

"Let's see."

For some reason, Joss looks at me again, even though Gentry's the one who dared her. I'm not sure if she's waiting for me to say something encouraging to her, but I don't. I unzip my backpack instead, take out my sketchbook and pencil. As she walks to the far side of the bowl, I start drawing.

There's no way I can keep up with her, though. That's obvious in the first couple of seconds. Joss toes the edge, and then down she goes—out of sight for a second or two, then up to the edge closest to us. She flips, heads back down. The board looks like it's part of her. Like she was born on it.

The next time she comes back up our side, she catches air. Even her hair defies gravity, all those curls dancing around her head as she disappears inside the bowl again and comes up the other side. She smiles as she grabs the side of her deck, catching even bigger air this time.

How can she smile so easy when I know for a fact that what she's doing is super hard?

Gentry's sitting next to me, making all kinds of noise like he's impressed.

After a minute, Joss comes back over to us, kicks her deck up into her hand. She's only a little out of breath. If I went down into that bowl even one time, I would have wiped out before I hit the bottom. I'd be totally deceased by now.

Gentry's sitting there with his mouth still open.

"Holy *what*?" he says. "That frontside one-eighty?? *Dude!*"

She just shrugs as I slurp the end of my Dragon Slayer.

Goes back and forth between me and Gentry a few times.

"So," she finally says. "What are we doing next?"

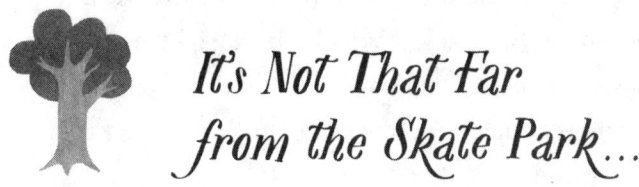

It's Not That Far from the Skate Park...

... to Gentry's house in Chapmantown, so we decide to walk it.

Joss takes sips off Gentry's Galaxy Fish while he acts like he's not saving it for her. A couple of times, I catch him going in for a micro-sip after her, probably so his lips can touch where her lips just touched. That's what I'd do. Closest thing to kissing a girl either of us have ever gotten.

Gentry's dad is in the kitchen when we get there, putting away the dishes he must've just washed. He looks like an aged-up version of Gentry's school picture from last year. Same hairstyle. Same goofy smile. Same blue eyes, like the water at Sycamore Pool on the sunniest day. Same shirt, now that I think about it. Gentry must've borrowed it from Sam for picture day.

"Hey, the whole posse's here," he says with a smile. Like the three of us are some kind of crew. Like we do this every Saturday. "What's the plan?"

"*Mario Kart*," Gentry says, leading the way to his room.

After a few minutes, Sam brings a plate of random food to us: cookies, pretzels, beef jerky—whatever was left at the tail end of a few different snack bags. He brings sodas, too, store-brand, but at least they're not expired.

We thank him, and after he leaves the room, Joss goes, "Your dad is so nice."

She's right. Sam is nice. How can he stay so nice when all life ever gave him was a ton of hard stuff to deal with? One time, I heard him tell Gentry, "It's no one's fault your mom died. But we have to make the best of what we still have."

Who thinks that way?

He even trusts us enough to leave us alone. One guy and two girls, unsupervised alone in Gentry's room, and no one's saying, *Leave the door open*. It's one thing if it's just me and Gentry, but Joss is here, too, and Sam isn't making it into some pervy thing. It's a nice switch from Jordan thinking everyone around him has pervy intentions, but that's probably just because he does.

Fun fact: Joss isn't just good at skateboarding. She kills at *Mario Kart* too.

"You know any of the cheats?" Gentry asks.

Joss goes, "*Pffft*. You don't need cheats. Just beat the staff ghosts so you can unlock the expert—"

"Yeah, I know," Gentry interrupts. "But I've never been able to do that. The cheats—"

She plunks the controller into her lap. "I thought you said you played this before."

"I have, but . . . how do you beat the ghosts without cheat codes?"

"Just watch. I'll show you."

They both lean to the left as they drift, then to the right. Gentry's way behind as they race through the track.

His game system only has two controllers, but I'm happy to sit on the floor and draw while they play. I capture Joss, smiling big with her hair flying around her, like when she was skating the bowl. My colored pencils are back at Gladys's, so I can't show the exact shade of light brown, but I can always add it in when I get home. Next, I sketch Gentry with sharp blast marks around him and all his teeth showing, nervous, like someone who's about to go down in flames. I notice how his hair is the same almost-white blond as the tips of Joss's hair—I make a mental note of that for later as I draw it in spikes to show him freaking out. With them sitting side by side, it's obvious how much taller Joss is. They're still talking about beating the ghosts, so that's what I surround them with—ghosts. Not the kind from the game of *Mario Kart*, but the kind from the game of actual life.

Except in actual life, there is no way to beat a

ghost. That's because ghosts don't have to be dead. My mom is a ghost, and she's in prison. The Silvas are ghosts, too, even though they're still in Oroville, living their best life with their surprise twins. Those babies would be about two by now, I realize with a zap of surprise.

Joss leans back after beating Gentry for the fifth time and grabs a fistful of pretzels off the plate. She drops them into her mouth one at a time from a few inches above her head. I can hear her chewing across the room.

Gentry pops open a soda and takes a long swig, burps it out at the end.

Joss spins around.

"Hey, how come you're always drawing stuff, but you never let anyone see?" she asks me.

I look between her and Gentry real quick. "I'm just a private person, I guess."

She nods. Rolls her skateboard back and forth under her feet. Turns to Gentry.

"You think you got the whole expert-ghost thing locked in?"

"Sure," he says. He's trying to sound like he's even, but I know a chipped ego when I hear one.

"Good," she says. "I expect a full report next time you beat your . . ." She looks around dramatically. "Brother? Sister?"

"It's just me and my dad," Gentry says. "He doesn't play too often."

Drago's sharp-toothed iris closes in around Joss. Drago and I both see what she's doing. She's digging for info without making it seem that way. And Gentry just took the bait. Why doesn't she just come out and ask him? I wonder.

"Is that how *you* got so good?" I ask her. "Playing against your . . . brother? Sister?"

She drops her eyeline for a second, grabs a broken cookie off the plate. "I'm just naturally skillful," she says after chewing for a bit.

Gentry and I make noises like we don't believe her. Then he asks, "So where did you go to school last year, anyway?"

"I didn't live here last year."

I go, "Where'd you live?"

"We moved up here from Santa Cruz. It's like three or four hours down the coast."

"Which do you like better?" Gentry asks.

She gives him some kind of side-eye. "Santa Cruz is on the *beach*, so . . ."

"Why'd your family move here, then?" Gentry asks as a text pings my phone.

I don't check to see who it is. I already know who it is. The only person besides Gentry who ever texts me.

A few seconds later it goes off again. I take a quick look—it's from Renée, not Gladys.

Will you be back soon? I could really use a little help with dinner.

I throw my stuff into my backpack and zip it closed.

"Where you going?" Gentry asks.

"I gotta get home. Can your dad drop me off?"

"I bet he can drop you both off."

Joss looks up, a half-eaten cookie puffing her cheek out.

"Oh," she says. "No, I . . . I'm good."

Gentry tosses the controllers under his TV stand. "You don't want a ride home?"

She shakes her head kind of hard. "I think I'm just . . . I'm gonna go skate some more."

"Yeah, but—"

"I'm solid," she says, hopping to her feet. "Totally solid."

She looks around like she can't find something, even though the only thing she had when we got here was her deck, and that's back under her arm already.

Gentry looks disoriented, and Joss just looks like she can't get out of there fast enough.

He goes, "Okay, well . . . you should come hang out again sometime. Kick my butt at *Mario Kart* some more. Or Ash. She's worse than I am."

"Don't drag me down in flames, just because you suck," I tell him.

Joss tosses her hair back. "Yeah," she says. "Cool."

When she reaches for the door, I think about how sometimes in class, she turns and looks at me, and it feels like she can see me, which is confusing. But this . . . isn't that. The way she's looking at me now has a different shape to it. A different mood.

The way she swings out the door without saying goodbye or anything.

Like she's hiding something.

Or keeping secrets.

Jordan's Sitting on the Couch...

...when I walk in. He's shooting zombies.

Again.

Still.

Gladys is shoving some kind of orange baby food into Marcus's mouth off a teeny-tiny spoon.

Renée's making dinner for the rest of us, because that's what she does on her one day off. Makes all the meals. Does all the laundry. Plays with Marcus, since she barely sees him the rest of the time.

"Hey, Renée," I say.

"Hey, Ash." Her words sigh into the kitchen. "Thanks for getting back here so quick. I just—"

"It's okay," I tell her. "I'll come help after I put my stuff away."

"That'd be great," she says, pushing hair out of her eyes with the back of her wrist.

I open the bedroom door, throw my backpack onto the bed. It stinks like dirty diapers in here, so

I pull the bag out of the trash pail. It weighs a ton, like maybe it hasn't been emptied in a while. Which is gross, because Marcus has a nasty rash and needs his diaper changed more than usual, not that they always do it. I make sure nothing's leaking and try not to let any part of the cram-packed bag touch my skin or clothes or drag on the floor as I lug it through the house and out to the cans. It takes some muscle to get it up over the side, but when I finally let it go, a blast wave of diaper stink explodes from inside the bin. It knocks me back a ways, makes my eyes water like crazy. For a few minutes, I just stand there, trying not to puke and wiping the tears away with my shirt, and when they finally clear up, that's when I see it.

Stumps. Two of them.

The rest of those two trees are lying on the ground in big chunks, waiting to be chopped into cordwood, it looks like. I shiver a little when I realize how close they are to my tree. I walk over, touch their rough-flat surfaces. Trace their rings inside. We learned about tree rings in fourth grade up in Oroville. Trees add a new one every year. You can track its age that way and learn about things that happened around it while it was growing.

What's wrong with these two trees that would make Jordan cut them down? They don't look sick, not even inside where the rings are. The thought sends a heavy feeling into my chest, something I don't have a name for. Why would anyone chop down a perfectly healthy tree when it's not even finished growing?

I break some kind of land-speed record running back to the house.

"Jordan!"

"Shut up! You're breaking my concentration!"

I pivot to Gladys, but she's pulling at Marcus's pants to smell if he made a dookie.

"Renée!" I shoot around the corner into the kitchen, all out of breath.

She spins away from the stove. "What's wrong? What happened?"

"Is Jordan cutting down *all* the trees?"

Her shoulders droop like a balloon someone let the air out of.

"Honey...I thought you got hurt or something." She shakes her head and mumbles, "I wish he wouldn't leave that chainsaw out there."

"Okay, but why is he chopping them down?"

She turns back to the stove.

"Why does he do anything, Ash?" she says with a sigh. "I guess you'll have to ask him yourself. Hand me those kidney beans. And the can opener."

"I'll do it." I clamp the can opener onto the lid and crank the handle. "Anyway, I already tried asking him, but he's too *busy* to answer." I aim that last part directly toward the living room.

But she doesn't say anything about me throwing

shade at Jordan. She just goes, "Ask him again, then. There should be an open thing of tomato paste in the fridge. Can you find that for me?"

"Hey, babe," Jordan calls out as the cries of dying zombies fly through the air. "Bring me a Coors."

My caseworker, Barbara, told Gladys she can have beer in the house if it's locked up, but this is Jordan's beer, and it's not supposed to be here because *he's* not supposed to be here. That's why he keeps an empty cooler in his truck. If it's time for a home visit, he just tosses them back there along with Marcus's Pack 'n Play before taking off.

"Babe!"

Renée flings the spoon she's using onto the counter.

"I swear . . . ," she says all the way under her breath, stepping away from the stove to get a Coors out of the fridge.

"I can bring it to him," I tell her, keeping my voice low. I feel my heart all the way through my bones and muscles—pounding so hard it fills my ears and so loud it nearly drowns out Jordan's zombie slaughter.

She hands me the bottle, and I curl my fingers around the skinny neck of it.

"Maybe don't mention the trees just now, actually." Renée's words sound funny in my ears, like she's talking underwater.

We lock eyes for a beat or two, and she doesn't look away till I nod. I know if I make Jordan mad, he'll take it out on her. He always takes it out on her, no matter who he's mad at.

I bring his precious beer into the living room, hold it out to him. He flips a glance from the bottle to my face.

"You gonna open it, or what?" he asks.

I crack the top open with the bottom of my shirt like it's zombie-Jordan's neck and hand it back to him. But I don't move. I know I should, because if I stay here, I'm going to say something about the trees, and I nod-promised to Renée that I wouldn't.

Jordan stares at me, beer in one hand, game controller in the other.

"What?" he snaps.

I swallow.

Once.

Twice.

Feel my mouth slowly open like it's not even attached to the rest of my body.

"Ash?" Renée calls from the kitchen, like she knows. "I could use an extra set of hands."

"*What?*" Jordan says again. "Don't just stand there. Go help her."

Back in the kitchen, Renée asks me to stir the chili con carne she threw together.

"I just need to make a simple salad real quick," she says.

While she chops up the lettuce hard and fast, I think about trees.

The small orchard of walnut trees in our yard.

The two that got cut down today that don't even look like they're sick.

My favorite climbing tree.

And a family tree that hurts every time I think about it.

On Monday Morning…

…I find Gentry just outside the gym, sitting on a bench under the word *COUGARS*. Right between the *U* and the *G*, just like always.

"How come you're late?" he says.

"I'm not *late*," I say. "I'm just . . . not early."

He nods and goes, "What happened this time?"

"Gladys didn't want to drive me today. She's like, 'It's only a couple of miles, Ash. You can walk. It won't kill ya.' Only she didn't call me Ash."

"She never does. So, wait, you walked all the way here?"

I nod.

"Maybe you should learn how to board? I bet Joss would teach you."

I hand him a slice of side-eye. "Yeah, right."

"I mean it. You saw her—she's really good—"

"I'm not gonna let Joss teach me how to

skateboard," I say. "I can figure it out on my own if I want. There's always TikTok."

"Oh, did you know she has a TikTok?"

Figures.

"Anyway," I say, "I don't have a skateboard, and it's not like Gladys would ever agree to get me one. Besides, it's probably against the rules."

"Is making you walk all that way to school and back against the rules too?" he says. "Cuz it should be."

He's right in some ways, but he also doesn't all the way get it. Sam is a lot more flexible than Gladys about things like getting to school. When Gentry's mom died four years ago, Sam transferred him to Citrus, which was only a block or so from his office, just so Sam could zip over and walk him back every day.

I shove my hands in my pockets, hear the crinkle of Ms. Kim's after-school reminder slip down at the bottom.

"Hey, are you going home right after school today?" I ask.

"I have to go to ACE until my dad gets out of his meeting."

"You keep talking about this ACE thing. What is it, anyway?"

"It stands for *After-Class Enrichment* or something like that."

"So it's like study hall."

"Well . . . we mostly play games and watch movies and stuff, so. It's better than study hall."

"Do you think your dad would give me a ride home after?"

"Yeah, but I'll be there till at least four thirty."

"What if I just come chill with you when I'm done in Ms. Kim's room?"

Gentry scoops his hair back with his fingers to get it the way he fixed it this morning and goes, "Text me when you're done, and I'll see if Mr. Yuan will let you in."

"Cool."

The first bell rings, so we grab our stuff and head to homeroom. I see Wiz and them shoving each other in the 200 wing, slamming into people and not even bothering to say they're sorry.

Gentry goes, "Jerks," under his breath.

"Did I tell you about Torres making Wiz my science partner?" I say.

Gentry makes a face like someone stepped on his foot.

He goes, "Have you ever smelled that guy?"

"Dude, I sit right next to him."

"No one wears that much Axe unless they're hiding something."

"Well, he stinks like pot too, so," I say, dropping to a whisper on the p-word. "That kid's got issues. Hey, what do you want to do at lunch?"

Gentry shrugs, opening the door to class. "Library? I need to work on something."

"Yeah," I say, leaving out the part about the assignment *I'm* supposed to work on. The family tree. The project I haven't even started yet. I wonder what would happen if I turned in the one Wiz and them made for me, and then snitched about it? Who would get in trouble—me or those guys?

I purposely walk past Miss Moua's desk on my way to my seat.

"Good morning, Ash," Miss Moua says.

"Hi. How's your baby?"

"He's fine. How's yours?"

"Okay. He has a really bad rash, though." I don't know why I said that, except that it's true, and if anyone would understand, it would be Miss Moua.

"Oh no," she says, looking genuinely concerned. "Do you know what they're doing to treat it?"

I freeze, because honestly, I don't think they *are* treating it. I'm pretty sure they don't change Marcus's diaper enough. But I don't really *know*-know anything, only that he's been waking up screaming for a few nights, probably because it hurts so bad.

"He just cries a lot," I say. "That's usually why, right?"

"Well, I'm happy to write down the name of the holistic cream I use. It works like a dream for diaper rash."

I don't know what *holistic* means, but it sounds like something expensive. I just nod and smile and go to my seat.

Gentry leans over as the tardy bell rings.

"What was *that* about?"

I turn to him, shrug, and shake my head like it's really nothing.

I could never explain to him how really not-nothing that conversation was. How it's really everything to have Miss Moua talk to me like I'm a person who can solve a problem instead of a person who *is* one.

Because that's what I've been since the day I was born.

A problem for my mom, because she'd barely aged out of foster care herself when she had me.

A problem because she had no money for us to live on, and because, once someone showed her how to cook meth, she didn't just get lost in selling drugs, she got lost in taking them too. I was still a problem after she got arrested, because she did have some, like, distant family, but no one was willing to take me. All they said was "That's what you get, Nicole," and cut her off from their lives completely. That's what she told me, anyway.

And I was a problem for seven other foster families before I met the Silvas when I was eight years old. Each family had their different reasons for letting me go.

Then I became a problem for the Silvas once their perfect family came along.

I was even a problem for Gladys, who they sent me to after the Silvas. "I was already fixin' to quit doing foster care," I heard her tell Barbara, my caseworker, through the phone. "I'm too damn old for this." Barbara begged her to reconsider. "We're desperate for a placement," she'd said.

Now I'm not just Gladys's problem, but Jordan's too.

So that's what I've been my whole life. Someone's problem.

And the truth is, if I make a real family tree, everyone's gonna know it.

At the Beginning of Fourth...

... **Mr. Mann shows us where** we should be in our family tree project by now.

I look down at the blank sheet of paper with only my name on it. I'm basically 99 percent behind.

Why do teachers do stuff like put up a schedule just so you can see how far behind you are and feel bad about it?

I bet Miss Moua would never do that.

Taryn Swisher raises her hand. "I have, like, four hundred cousins. No, seriously, I do," she adds when people start to drag her for being all dramatic about it. "I'm just saying, I don't know how I'm supposed to fit everyone on there. I don't even know most of their names."

"See me after class with any specific issues," Mr. Mann says, not to Taryn, but to whoever. Then he goes off about dynasties and empires and how far those families extended. I'm not sure if this is his lesson today or just a rant, but it goes on long enough for me to decide I'm probably in trouble if I was supposed to write any of it down, because I didn't.

I wonder what would happen if I explained my situation to him. Would he let me do a different assignment? Some teachers don't even give this family tree project in social studies. You *can* study dynasties without it.

But then, as if he thinks he's making a joke, he goes, "Some of these dynasties were enormous, yet somehow"—he looks directly at Taryn Swisher—"people managed to document and record them for posterity."

That's when I decide he wouldn't be cool enough about it for me to tell him anything personal.

Man, I wish it was time for this class to end. Except lunch comes next, and after what happened on Friday, I'm dreading it.

Gentry texts me the second the bell rings at the end of fourth.

Enriquez gave me lunch detention.
What for?
I called Matt Adams a jerk.
Why'd she give you detention for that?
Cuz that's not the word I used.

That would be funny, except Gentry being in lunch detention means I'll be alone, and that's one of the worst times to be alone around here.

Gtg, he texts. *See you at ACE.*

There's no way I'd go the cafeteria alone today. I stick with the original plan to go to the library, plant myself at a table, and pull my hoodie up so no one bugs me.

Just when I get out my sketchbook and pencils, Joss slides into the spot Gentry would be in, if it wasn't for Matt Adams being such a jerk. Or whatever scandalous word Gentry used.

"Where's G?" she asks.

G . . . ?

"Uh . . . serving detention," I say.

She doesn't nod or anything. She just says, "So, how come you're in here?"

"How come *you* are?" I ask. "It's not like anyone would ever do anything bad to *you* in the caf."

Joss rolls her eyes, snorts a little. "How would you even know?"

I stare at her. Because I kind of *do* know. I know how easy kids like her have it. What could someone like her possibly have to worry about? She's cool. She's cute. She's got mad skills. She could literally go anywhere she wants at lunch, and no one would give her crap. I mean, when was the last time someone spread a photoshopped picture of *her* around campus? Kids like Joss own places like middle school.

I skep-squint at her. "So you just came to the library today because you're bored of the caf?"

"No," she says. "I'm just . . . It's whatever."

Which is kind of how she left Gentry's on Saturday too. But I guess I'm not just *whatever* today. I'm tired of being just *whatever*.

I cram my stuff back into my backpack and shove my chair away from the table. And even though I hate doing it, I walk away from Joss Cruz.

There's a Sub...

...**in PE, as if the ongoing torture** of dressing out in the locker room wasn't bad enough.

Why is there a sub already? It's barely the second week of school.

"You can call me Mrs. Paul." She snaps her words like she's already mad at us.

"What's your *real* name?" Matt Adams shouts.

Some of the class laughs, but she ignores him. Why do so many teachers ignore guys like Matt and Wiz when I know for a fact that if I blurted out something like that, I'd have double-detention for life?

Someone asks, "Where's Coach Miller?"

But instead of answering, the sub goes, "Today we're collaborating with Mr. Carter's class. Gentlemen, you will go with Mr. Carter as soon as they show up. Ladies, you'll stay with me."

Good riddance to Wiz and them, I silently say as Mr. Carter's class wanders in.

There are a few minutes of confusion while the boys from our class spill down onto the gym floor and the girls from Mr. Carter's class climb up. Apparently, Joss is in that class. She keeps her eyes on me as she heads to the top of the bleachers.

"I bet we're gonna talk about our periods," Cassie Knowles says.

The girl next to her snorts and goes, "*Are You There, God? It's Me, Margaret,*" which gets a good laugh, because we all know we read that book in like fourth or fifth grade, whether we admit it or not.

I don't laugh, though. Part of me is waiting for someone to ask why I'm still here. *I thought the boys are supposed to go with Mr. Carter.*

The girl in front of me bumps the girl next to her with her elbow and points up. I look up, too, noticing the mural of a cougar bursting through the ceiling for the first time. Now I realize why there are odd patches of beige paint on the gym floor, outlined in black—they're supposed to be pieces of the ceiling knocked out by the cougar.

This is a bad omen. I knew it. I knew the sky was going to fall in PE one day—I just never thought it would be this soon.

Mrs. Paul blows a short burst on her whistle.

"I want everybody to head out and gather on the Oleander side of the yard."

As we make our way outside toward Oleander Avenue, I hear a few girls talking about the cemetery just across the blacktop from where we're headed.

Who puts a school next to a cemetery?

Mrs. Paul comes around and stands in front of us with her hands on her hips. She clears her throat, holds her hand up like she's making a peace sign, and goes, "Two words: Zombie. Apocalypse."

Some girls giggle because she accidentally flips the bird while counting off the two things, but the sound quickly fizzles out when she doesn't react. Her gaze bounces against our silence like a rogue ping-pong ball, until someone mumbles, "Are you telling a joke?"

Cassie Knowles goes, "Uh. Zombies are dead."

"Yeah, the apocalypse is over. The zombies won."

Laughter scatters across the faded blacktop.

But Mrs. Paul seems determined to not be bucked off her zombie horse.

She says, "In every apocalypse movie, in fact in *any* story where there's an epic battle of good versus evil, one thing happens consistently, every time. Something that helps save humanity. Anyone know what it is?"

I let out a silent groan inside my head. This is not going to end well for the sub.

"Anyone?"

"The grown-ups always die first, and the kids have to fix everything."

"The prettiest girl trips and falls right in front of the zombies and can't get back up."

"Don't worry—zombies are only interested in brains, so. You'd be safe."

A few girls laugh at that.

"Someone invents *Call of Duty* so you can kill all the—"

Mrs. Paul blows her whistle. "That's enough."

Kendalyn Meyer says, "Well, you asked," but she ignores that.

She stares us down like she's photographically memorizing our faces.

"So, what's the answer?" Taryn Swisher asks.

After another dramatic pause, the sub says, "There's always . . . an escape scene."

The class erupts in a chorus of groans.

"That's so cringe!" the girl behind me whispers, and whoever's next to her goes, "I know, right?"

"Are you gonna teach us parkour moves? Cuz that would be cool."

Even though I can't see her, I know by the edge in the voice that Joss is the one asking the parkour question.

Mrs. Paul walks around behind these concrete-barricade-looking things. Two of them are about waist high, the other two about chest high. We drive past them every morning just before we pull into the school's drop-off zone, but I've never even thought about what they were for.

The sub hasn't peeled her eyes off us, not even to blink, and she keeps on staring as she strikes a kind of pose before taking the most minuscule running start in history and flinging herself against the side of the shorter wall. But she does make it over, and raises her arms in a victory pose on the other side.

"Does that mean you're a zombie?" Taryn Swisher says, and the entire class busts out laughing. I try not to, but I can't help giggling a tiny bit.

It takes a few seconds for Mrs. Paul to catch her breath, and once she does, she bends down, opens her gym bag, and pulls out the clipboard that has the roll sheet on it.

"Everyone ready?" she asks.

"Ready for what?" Taryn Swisher asks back.

"For your big escape scene."

And just like that, no one's laughing anymore.

Things I Can't Do...

...not in any specific order:

I can't run fast.

I can't swim very well.

And I can't jump over things.

So I'm not gonna stand here and pretend like I'm not freaking out.

I'm totally freaking out.

Mrs. Paul splits the class in half and has us line up by the two shorter walls.

"The idea is to make it over the wall without falling, slipping, or ricocheting off."

More groans.

"And your *goal*"—she pulls hard on the word—"is to land upright on the other side of the wall and hold your position for five seconds, in order for the jump to count."

"Not *my* goal," I mumble under my breath.

The girl next to me whispers, "Right?"

"Once you've mastered the shorter wall," the sub calls out, "you'll move to the taller wall. You must master *both* walls before we can move on."

Wait, *what* . . . ?

"What happens if we can't do it?" Kendalyn Meyer asks.

"The rest of the class will run laps until you can."

The second after she says it, my brain explodes, and then one of the girls from Mr. Carter's class goes, "Are you *serious*?" and suddenly everyone is arguing with the sub about how cringe-to-the-power-of-unfair this is.

But Mrs. Paul just barks at us to line up behind the walls. Some of the girls stand there with their arms crossed, throwing weapons-grade shade at her. No one's excited about this. I'm personally terrified.

I count how many girls are lined up in front of me and realize—I'm unlucky number thirteen.

A few girls nail the short wall on their first try and move on. Some do exactly what Mrs. Paul said—they sort of make it but don't land solid on their feet, or they bounce against the side and fall backward onto the ground. Mrs. Paul tells them to go to the end of the line and try again.

My heart slams the inside of my chest over and over and over.

I count again.

Eight ahead of me.

Seven.

Four.

I'm next.

I hate knowing I'm being watched.

When it's my turn, Mrs. Paul shouts out crits about my form, loud enough for everyone to hear. Then she comes over, puts a hand on my shoulder. I think it's for encouragement at first, until she starts to press down.

"Bend your elbows," she says. "Make your knees more supple."

I side-eye her. What does it even mean to *make my knees more supple*?

When I finally jump, it looks more like I'm throwing myself at the wall.

"Back of the line," Mrs. Paul says.

"But—"

"Back."

"—can't I just—"

"*Go.*"

She watches me drag myself to the back of the line like she's making sure I don't run off, then pivots to the girl whose turn it is.

The next time I'm up again, there are only eight other people in line with me. Everyone else has moved on.

After my third try, there are only four of us.

Then it's just me.

One by one, the rest of the girls jump the higher

wall. I try to block out the sound of them counting off the five seconds for the jump to be considered good, and the cheer that follows.

Now they're all just sitting around. Watching me. Watching me try to jump the first decrepit wall again. Still.

"Everybody up!" Mrs. Paul calls out after what's probably my eighty-seventh try. "Laps."

A storm of "*What?*s" and "*No fair!*s" scatters across the blacktop as the sub points them in the direction she wants them to go.

I turn to run with the rest of the class.

"Not you," Mrs. Paul says. "They'll run until you're finished."

"*Seriously?*"

But she just goes, "*Zombies*. Think of those girls as zombies, and if you don't make it over the top of the wall like the rest of your team, you'll die."

"Why are you encouraging me to give in to peer pressure?" I ask, but she acts like she doesn't hear me.

"Loosen up," she says. "Get out of your own head."

I watch the rest of the class as they fake-jog across the blacktop. Cringe at their miserable faces going by.

"Think of your lower half as shock absorbers—"

"That's not helping," I tell Mrs. Paul.

She makes a face like *Well, fine, then* and backs away while pretending to look at her clipboard. Meanwhile, the rest of the class comes around the perimeter and passes by me.

"Thanks a lot, Ash," Taryn Swisher says.

"Just jump the freakin' wall," Kendalyn Meyer whines.

Joss turns her head after she goes by, watches me for a second or two before looking forward again.

Now that their backs are to me, I try again. I do. I try. This time, my knees hit the side of the wall. The sub is pretending to ignore me, but some of the girls openly glare at me as they jog.

I try again.

And again.

No help from Mrs. Paul.

Nothing but harsh looks and words from everyone else.

As the class comes back around, Joss peels away from the group.

"She didn't say *we* couldn't help you," she announces.

"I've never been good at jumping," I panic-whisper. "Till now."

My face feels kind of crumbly. I go, "*What?*"

"You've never been good at jumping, *until now*," she says again.

". . . Oh-kay."

"Which do you think is more important for this—upper-body strength or lower-body strength?"

It feels like a trick question, so I go against my instincts and say, "Um . . . upper?"

"Lower, actually. But it's not as hard as she's

making it out to be. You just have to . . . kind of . . . plant your left foot on the wall. Like this." She shows how she rests her foot on top of the ledge, then follows the jump through. "That'll give you . . . like . . . safety as the other leg carries your momentum forward."

I look at the wall again, still skeptical. She shifts her whole body to one side like she's figuring out how else to explain it to me.

"Think of it like . . ." Her eyes roll upward. "Okay. How would you draw someone getting on a horse?"

"Huh. I . . . well . . . I'd . . . put one foot in the stirrup . . . like this." I prop my foot up about midway on the wall.

"What next?"

"I'd . . . um . . . put their hands on the saddle." I grasp the top of the wall with my fingers. "And then . . . maybe draw arrows . . . showing the cowgirl going up and over." I awkward-laugh at the end because I added a cowgirl to her story.

"Can you see it?" she asks.

"I mean . . . yeah."

"Okay, so . . . visualize it." She blinks at me, shakes her hair back behind her, blinks again. "Be the cowgirl."

Four tries later, I'm wobbling on the other side of the wall. Joss *woot*s so loud, the rest of the class turns. Some of the girls cheer.

A couple say things like "It's about time!" and

"Finally!" but a lot of them seem genuinely happy I made it.

Mrs. Paul looks like she's deciding whether to still make me do the other wall, but the dress-down bell rings before she gets the chance to.

And Joss just goes, "See? You've never been good at jumping *until now*."

I feel myself smile.

I never thought about the power two small words could have.

Until now.

Someone Calls Out My Name...

. . . **as I leave PE.**

I ignore it. But then Joss trots up beside me.

"Hey," she breathes. "Didn't you hear me?"

I shrug. "Sometimes people yell things just to get in my head."

"Gotcha," she says. "So. Where ya going?"

"I'm supposed to go see Ms. Kim."

"Can I walk with you?"

I sneak a quick look at her. She's not smiling, but she's not *not* smiling either.

"I guess."

"Cool."

She drops her skateboard on the ground and hangs on to the strap of my backpack like I'm her personal tugboat. Not that I mind.

"Why do you have to go see Ms. Kim, anyway?" she asks.

"To finish her stupid free write."

She looks a little surprised, but she just goes, "The one where you're supposed to say what she should know about you? Why do teachers always ask that question?"

"Because they know you'd never tell them anything personal if they didn't."

She snorts. "Maybe it's a sly teacher way of getting you to make up stories without letting you think you're doing creative writing."

She uses air quotes for the last two words, and we both laugh. Joss probably laughs because it's pretty funny. I laugh because it's actually kind of smart.

We're almost at the end of the main hallway when I ask, "So . . . why'd you help me in PE, anyway?"

She goes, "That sub was a turd."

"She totally was." I laugh again, but it sounds weird, so I stop, which also sounds weird. I hate being a weirdo. I wish I knew some other way to be.

Joss leans in like she's about to tell me some huge secret, and when she does, some of her hair gets caught in a puff of breeze and blows into my face. She doesn't seem to notice.

"I didn't know you were going to be in the library today," she tells me. "But I was glad you were because . . . I just don't trust those guys, y'know? So when I saw you there . . . I dunno. I just wanted to see if you were okay."

"Why did *you* go to the library instead of the caf?" I ask.

She adjusts herself on her skateboard, shifts her weight a little. "Sometimes I just get annoyed with people," she says without elaborating.

I kind of don't want the conversation to end, but also, we've walked all the way to Ms. Kim's room, and I probably only have a minute to get inside.

The silence is every kind of awkward.

"Okay, well . . ." Joss lets go of my backpack strap. "See you later, Ash."

For some nerdy reason, I say, "If you're lucky."

She laughs—the kind of laugh that sounds easy.

"You're such a dork!" she says.

But she's still laughing.

I made Joss Cruz laugh.

I want to carry that feeling with me, except now I have to go inside and finish my essay about what I want Ms. Kim to know about me.

And then I realize . . .

Joss knew exactly which free write I was talking about. Why would she know that, unless she hated answering the question as much as I did?

Now all I can wonder about is what she doesn't want Ms. Kim to know about *her*.

She Never Said...

... how long it had to be. She hasn't said *anything*, just points to the desk right in front of her and goes back to whatever she was doing on the computer.

I take out my paper. *What I Want Ms. Kim to Know About Me ...*

I spin a pencil between my fingers a few times. Then I bend forward and start writing.

I don't like sharing my personal thoughts and feelings.

I don't like writing assignments, especially this one.

I don't like staying late because no one will come get me when it's over, and it's a long way to walk.

"I'm done," I tell her.

She looks surprised when her eyes come away from the computer.

She goes, "I bet you have a little more to say. Keep going."

I have nothing else to say, so instead I start drawing. I draw Drago vanquishing the evil, three-faced Ms. Kim impersonator.

That'll teach you! Drago says inside a talking bubble. *Never pretend to be a teacher for your nefarious reasons, ever again!*

It takes a while to get all the details right. When I'm done, I hand it to her, and the real Ms. Kim says, "Good. Thanks for coming in, Ash." She takes the paper without even looking at it.

I bet she'll be upset about my new drawing. She'll probably say I still didn't give a real answer to her question.

I'm also pretty sure I don't care anymore.

Done, I text as I walk toward the 500 wing.

Gentry shoots back, *Get over here quick so I can deal u in.*

Deal me in? Like in *poker*?

When I get to room 500, I peek through the open door until I get Gentry's attention, and I hear him ask, "Mr. Yuan. Can I go get my friend?"

Within one second of Mr. Yuan saying "Sure," Gentry comes skidding into the hallway.

"I love that guy—he's the chillest dude in the universe," he says, shoving me back inside. He pushes me right past the teacher, toward a cluster of desks at one end of the room.

We almost make it, but Mr. Yuan calls out to him.

"Hey, whoa. Aren't you going to introduce me to your friend?"

"Yeah. Um. This is Ash."

"Hi, Ash," Mr. Yuan says with a big smile. "Come over here so we can make you official for today."

I look back at Gentry the same way Gladys's dog Frampton used to look at her whenever Jordan would yell at him just for being a dog. That is, before Animal Control showed up at the house. Jordan says one of the neighbors snitched on him for hitting that dog with a branch from one of the walnut trees, and it turned out Jordan wasn't even supposed to be near dogs anymore. He's considered a "serial abuser." Frampton was a good boy—he didn't deserve to be yelled at or hit. And I felt bad for Gladys that her dog got taken away. They should have taken Jordan away instead.

"So, listen," Mr. Yuan says. "You're always welcome to stop in if you're having a tough day or something. If you want to join ACE officially, there's a few other steps you'll have to take first, so just let me know. Okay?"

I swallow. "Okay."

Now I really do feel like I'm not supposed to be here. Like when I went to live with the Manfredis. Then the Fitches. Foster families who already had kids. Who already had their ways of doing everything. Going to baseball practice. Going to church. Going to bed at a certain time. And then I show up, and I don't know any of the rules. I don't know if I can trust anyone. Or what will happen if I do or say the wrong thing, because I don't know the right way to do anything in that family. And a lot of times, I'd get in trouble anyway.

And now it seems like everyone's staring at me too. I dip my chin over my shoulder again, searching for Gentry. One look at my face and he zips across the room to see what's going on, only everything's happening in slo-mo, and I can't really hear anything over the ringing in my head.

But Mr. Yuan just has me sign in and then hands me a guest pass. I shove it into my pocket, and Gentry pulls me by the sleeve back to the cluster of desks as my head-noise dials down a little bit.

"Henry won," some kid in a *Vote for Pedro* shirt tells him. "You had crappy cards—I looked."

I sit down and Gentry slides into the seat next to me. "It's called Shattered! Want to play?"

I shake my head and whisper, "I'll just watch."

I really don't like doing new things around people I don't know. Like those wall jumps in PE. And once I start thinking about the walls, I slip right back into that same feeling I had in gym class—everyone watching, thinking I'm an even bigger loser than they did before—and it's harder than ever to breathe.

When the *Vote for Pedro* kid starts setting out a new round of cards, I sneak a look around the room.

There's one whole wall of nothing but these tall gray cabinets. Another long wall that's all windows, with thick purple curtains. There's even a stagelike area off to the side of the room with a wall clock high above it. According to the clock, it's barely three thirty. Gentry said he'd be here till at least four thirty. I'm not sure if I can sit here, fighting to catch my breath, feeling like I'm right back in front of those zombie apocalypse walls, for almost another hour.

Mr. Yuan sits with his feet up on the teacher's desk and pretends he's not watching us, but he is. I can tell.

The noise at the Shattered! table gets louder as the game goes on. I tune it out as much as I can. The jokes. The pretend accusations of cheating. The agonized groans when someone draws a bad card or loses a turn.

Suddenly, Gentry shouts, "Demolished!" and the other kids slap a stack of cards on the table. The kid with his hand on top calls Gentry an inappropriate name.

"Keep it nice!" Mr. Yuan warns from his desk.

"How come you're not playing with us?" Mónica Ramirez asks Mr. Yuan.

"I'm strategizing how to win against Dominic." He taps his head. "I'll only let someone beat me once."

The kids playing Shattered! laugh at the inside joke. Gentry fist-bumps Dominic, but only Gentry explodes his at the end, his jellyfish tentacles coming into my airspace for a second.

I put my hoodie up and pull the strings tight until there's just enough of an opening to look at the clock again.

Three thirty-nine.

My heart thrashes inside me. Then all the sound in the room goes stretchy in my ears. I know what this means. I know what's happening. And I don't want people to see me like this—having what the Silvas told me was a panic attack when it happened in their home and I didn't know what to call it.

But I can't make it stop, and I don't want to do that here.

I lean in close to Gentry.

"Hey," I whisper. "I think I'm gonna go."

I feel bad about how surprised he looks when he turns.

He goes, "What do you mean? I thought we were giving you a ride home."

"No, it's cool. I'll walk."

"But . . . my dad's coming—"

"I just feel like walking. Okay?" The words come out way sharper than I ever meant them to.

He leans away from me, but his eyes never move off my face.

His "Okay" doesn't even sound like his voice.

I look at the rest of the Shattered! group before coming back around to him.

"I'll catch you tomorrow," I say.

"Yeah. Sure."

The last thing I see in room 500 is Gentry, slumped down in his seat.

The first thing I see outside room 500 is Joss.

Leaning against a post at the other end of the hall.

Looking in my direction.

I'm Not Feeling Back to Normal...

...but for some reason Joss standing at the other end of the hallway at least makes me feel a little less panicky.

"What are you doing here?" I ask.

"I was just—Are you okay?"

I shake my head, and she goes, "Dang, Ash, sit down for a minute."

She offers me her skateboard to sit on.

"Breathe," she says. "All the way into your diaphragm." She points to the area between her rib cage and belly button.

I feel my lungs filling with air instead of fighting for it, so I take another deep breath, then another, and I feel a shade better each time.

"Thanks."

"Where were you going, anyway?" she asks.

"I dunno. Home, I guess."

"Which way is that?"

I pull my hoodie down, run my fingers through my hair to unflatten it a little.

"Up the Esplanade," I say.

I try to point, but my hand is too shaky, so I use it to wipe away some sweat from under my nose.

"Can I walk with you? I mean . . . I probably can't go the whole way, but maybe part of the way?"

I cut a quick look at her.

"I guess."

Joss takes the lead—across the blacktop where the walls we jumped in PE today loom off to the left. The cemetery is ahead and to the right, partly walled off by a row of trees and bushes. I don't say anything when she heads in that direction, or when she finds an opening in the chain-link fence.

Once we're inside the cemetery, Joss reaches behind her and slides her skateboard through the straps of her backpack so she doesn't have to carry it.

"My grandma's buried here somewhere," she says out of the blue.

I look at her again. "She is?"

"Yeah." The sounds of traffic take over the conversation until she goes, "My abuela was awesome. I used to come stay with her every summer when we lived in Santa Cruz, but then—" She cuts that thought off quick and just finishes with "I really miss her."

I nod so she knows I hear her, not to say I understand. Because I don't. I can't—I mean . . . I never even knew my mom's mom. "I'm not gonna leave you forever like *my* mom did, baby girl," my mom told me when I was five and Barbara brought me to see her in jail. "I'm gonna get better, too, I swear. I'll get clean. I'm not gonna die on you like that and leave you without a family." But she'd already lost her family. All of them. Mostly when she was my age and her mom died. And then after—when she was pregnant with me at seventeen, and the few aunts and cousins she had left were like, "You brought this on yourself, Nicole," and "You're definitely your mother's daughter." So when it turned out she needed someone to raise me just like her mom had needed someone to raise her, there was no grandma to help her out, and no one in the family stepped up.

So no. I don't know what it's like to have a grandma. And I'm not sure what to say when someone talks about a person they lost. The best I can come up with is "Was she your mom's mom or your dad's mom?"

The way Joss doesn't answer feels kind of weird. Like I'm not supposed to ask. Or for sure like she doesn't want to answer.

The paved path we've been walking down turns into a dirt path, and the conversation goes completely cold. It stays that way for long enough to officially be awkward.

And then it hits me.

"Hey, how are you doing on that project for Mann's class, anyway?"

"I haven't even started." She sounds like she's dreading it as much as I am.

I look down where the sidewalk comes to an end, as we wait to cross at the light on First and Mangrove.

We keep going, past the take-and-bake pizza place, past the Popeyes that smells so good it makes my stomach growl. I wait until we hit the Harley-Davidson shop on the corner of Fifth before I swallow hard and try cracking into the silence again.

"I . . . Wiz and them made me a family tree."

She looks at me hard as we walk, her eyes kind of narrow all of a sudden. "What do you mean? What kind of family tree?"

"You know. Unicorns. Jeffree Star. RuPaul."

She stops and turns. Her mouth pops open.

"Are you kidding me?"

I shake my head no.

"Apparently, Megan Rapinoe is my aunt. I guess that explains my mad soccer skills." I mean it as a joke, but it doesn't sound like one, and it doesn't land on Joss that way either.

She makes a face I've never seen before. Anger. With zero filter.

"What a bunch of *jerks*. You know . . . those are the kind of guys who try to kiss you just because you danced with them *one time* at the Valentine's Dance. It's called consent, y'know? And you don't *owe* it to anyone."

I definitely hit a nerve.

"Yeah, I'm really glad you're not friends with them," I confess.

"Uh, no. I don't have any friends." She tosses her hair around behind her, and I keep staring at her, waiting to see if *she's* making a joke.

But she's not.

"You have friends," I say.

"Nope."

"Those girls you sit with in the cafeteria—"

"Nobody has friends in middle school, Ash," she tells me. "There are people you sit with at lunch so they won't beat you up. And people you just avoid. That's all."

Her words crash around in my head as her phone pings a message notification.

Joss reaches into her back pocket, reads the message, replies, then goes, "You know, Mr. Mann could teach us about dynasties and stuff without making us do a pointless family tree."

I'm still trying to figure out what to say about her *friends* comment when Joss slides the phone back into her pocket.

"Okay, well." She sticks out her thumb in the complete opposite direction of where I live. "I'm going that way."

"Okay. Cool."

"Thanks for letting me crash your walk," she says. "See ya tomorrow."

"Yeah. See ya."

The rest of the way home feels like a kaleidoscope. Taking in all the tiny parts people see about me that don't make up a whole picture of my life. Thinking about all the broken bits of things Joss has said and done that don't make up a whole picture of hers. How she didn't want Gentry's dad to drive her home on Saturday. How she wouldn't tell me if her grandma was her mom's mom or her dad's mom. How it seems like she hates the family tree assignment as much as I do. Not to mention her reaction to Ms. Kim's writing assignment.

When you look at something through a kaleidoscope, all you see is the chaos of it.

Now I'm wondering what Joss's world looks like without all that shatter.

The Sound of Wood Splitting...

...**hits me before I** make it around the last corner.

I detour out of the road and sneak through the overgrowth so Jordan can't see me. Only he's not alone. His friend Kenny is with him.

And they're swinging their axes at the tree next to mine.

Chipping at the branches.

Chopping off the limbs.

All that's left now is a straight up-and-down trunk with nothing holding on to it.

They're laughing.

Two longneck beers sit on an upright log a few feet away from them.

Jordan takes one last swing at the tree, then sinks his axe into the stump he uses as a base for chopping cordwood. He picks up both beers, holds one out to Kenny.

"You remember that time we took the quads out

with Hunter and them?" Kenny says, dropping his axe next to Jordan's hard enough to make the other one wobble. He grabs the beer, takes a long swig.

"Out there by Black Butte Lake?" Jordan asks. "Where we met those girls?"

"Yeah! Okay, so . . . remember that one girl? The redhead?"

Only they both say *the redhead* at the same time.

Jordan goes, "Hell yes! I definitely remember that girl."

I hate the way they're both smiling.

Jordan asks, "What was her name, anyway?"

"Shayna," Kenny says. "Did I tell you I ran into her recently?"

"*No*. Where?" Jordan lifts his beer again, takes a long drink as Kenny tells him, "Down at Riley's."

"Bro, what're you doing going to *Riley's* for?" He wipes his mouth with the back of his hand. "That's a college bar, man."

"Exactly." Kenny's smile has way too much teeth to it. He looks gross.

I dip down, pull two shrub branches apart to get a better look.

Kenny peeks into his beer with one eye closed as he swirls it around.

"Anyway, there she was. So, I tried to get her to talk to me, but it was like she didn't even recognize me or something."

"Serious?" Jordan says.

"Man, that girl wouldn't give me the time of day."

"She doesn't owe you the time of day," I blurt.

Jordan and Kenny both stop what they're doing like they're playing freeze tag. Then they turn.

"Ash, what in the hell are you doing over there?" Jordan says, his ears turning all kinds of red like they do when he gets mad.

Kenny goes, "Looks like she's spying to me."

I push the branches and weeds out of my way and take a few careful steps closer to them, but not too close.

"Girls don't owe you their time," I say again. "They don't owe you anything. Not even if they already let you dance with them. It's called consent."

Jordan snaps, "Get in the house."

But I'm not talking to Jordan. I'm talking to Kenny. And I'm not done.

"Also," I say, "you don't get to be mad at her about it either. Those are the rules."

Jordan's whole face is fiery red by now.

"Ashley, I said, *get in the house*! *Now!*"

My focus on Kenny snaps. I'm frozen in place, realizing too late how stupid it was to pop off to Jordan's friend right in front of him. Even though I can't unsay those things now, and even though Kenny totally deserved it.

But still.

Jordan's standing there, madder than ever, yelling at me to go inside when I'm frozen and can't move, and now all I see is that axe in the stump, and I'm not sure what he'd try to do with it, even with Kenny just a few feet away.

Kenny's eyes flip from me to Jordan.

Jordan's eyes are blazing all over me.

I unplant my feet somehow and peel away from them real quick, away from the stumps and the logs and the axes.

I go straight into the house.

Straight into my room.

No one has to tell me not to come out the rest of the night.

I'm way too scared of Jordan right now to even think about going back out there.

Not even if they told me I had to.

Around the Time the Sun Starts to Set...

...Gladys knocks on the door to say it's time for dinner.

"I'm not hungry," I call back, relieved that she doesn't force me to come out.

All she says is "That's your choice," only it doesn't sound very understanding.

At bedtime, she's back, this time to put Marcus down. She doesn't say anything about me missing dinner. She just looks at me strangely without saying anything at all.

It could be because I'm on the floor, crammed between my bed and the wall, fully dressed, holding on to my backpack like a shield.

Out in the living room, Jordan has plenty to say. I can hear him from in here.

He rants about how disrespectful I am. How disgusting I am. How not-worth-it this all is. As if he's in charge. As if it's his decision to foster me, and not Gladys's.

Gladys does everything she can to reason with him. But she never tells him he has to calm down or leave, the way she should.

She just goes, "If I give her up now, you'll have to get a job, Jordy. I'm not kidding. I'll kick you out, and you won't have me to take care of you and the baby no more."

"Don't go making empty threats," he says.

"Nothing empty about it. And don't think I'm just gonna go out and get another kid. I've had it. I'm done."

"At least you wouldn't have to deal with a little baby-dyke, now, would you?"

His words shatter the air. Broken bits falling all around me.

"Nothing you can do about that either," Gladys says. "So don't even try. I know that look of yours, Jordy. You can't touch that kid, or this is all over."

I stare at my shoes as they talk.

I mean.

As Jordan yells and Gladys talks.

I stare at my shoes wondering how far away they can take me before they fall apart.

. . . Or I do.

Marcus rolls over in his Pack 'n Play crib and whimpers. The sound of the TV on low mumbles from down the hallway. Jordan and Gladys talking over it. Talking about me again. Still.

I check the time on my phone. It's just after nine o'clock, which I know is late to ask someone if you can come over on a school night. And I know when I left Gentry at ACE today, he didn't seem too happy about it. But none of that seems as important right now as getting out of here. Not with Jordan out there acting like a stick of dynamite and talking about me like *I'm* the match.

Hey, I text to Gentry. *Can I come over?*

The little dots pulse.

You mean, now? he types.

Yeah, it's urgent. Would your dad come get me?

The screen goes dead. No dots. No pulse.

Nothing.

And then . . .

He says okay.

Can he wait on the corner? I don't think he should come right up to the house tonight.

A beat later, Gentry types: *Sure.*

As soon as I read that last word, I start to feel relieved. Until I realize that meeting them on the corner means sneaking out of the house. And sneaking out of the house is going to mean doing something brave.

Almost like . . .

Like a big escape scene. Like escaping the zombie apocalypse.

My head tilts up until the window is in view. It's not nearly as high as the wall I jumped in PE.

The wall . . . *I jumped* . . . in PE.

I never would have thought about doing something like this in my entire life.

Until now.

I Always Figured...

...**the reason they told** me to keep the window shut in this room is because the screen always fell out. And that Jordan must have gotten so sick of Gladys barking at him about finding the screen on the ground outside, he finally fixed it.

It turns out, Jordan's way of "fixing" it was to nail the whole window shut.

I bet that nail wasn't there when we moved in, or we probably never would have passed our home inspection with Children's Services.

Now I look around in a panic. There has to be something in here to pull a nail up with. I search my backpack, my dresser, even Marcus's diaper bag. Nothing. Even if I could sneak into the rest of the house to look for something I could use, Jordan traded all his tools for that Xbox he always plays.

I check the time on my phone again. It's about a twelve-minute drive across Chico from Chapman-town where Gentry lives. If I'm doing the math right,

I have about seven minutes before he and his dad are on the corner.

I go back to the window, squint in the dark so I can see the nail a little better. It's bent. Like someone hammered it in, then bent it into an L shape on purpose. But that could actually work better, because all I need is something to leverage against it, and it should pop right out. I only know that because we did a Principles of Physics unit last year, just before the Intro to Quantum Physics one.

My backpack starts to slide off my shoulder, so I heft it back into place, and that's when I hear the sound of my key chain collection tinkling softly. I swing the backpack off, grab the two longest key chains—a guitar from Hard Rock Cafe that Gentry brought me back from vacation this summer, and a wooden surfboard I bought at a yard sale for a nickel. Since the guitar is made of metal, that's the one I stick under the nailhead. Then I use the surfboard to gently pry it upward. I love that surfboard, but also, it would be perfectly fine if I had to sacrifice it for the cause. I switch between prying the nail with the guitar and wiggling it with my fingers until it feels like it's coming loose. I can tell I'm really close, when suddenly my phone starts blowing up.

I stop to look. It's Gentry.

We're here—where are you?

Stuck inside. Gimme a minute, I write back.

Hurry.

That's not helpful, I think, going back to prying. I hear the wooden surfboard grunt from the pressure.

"C'mon," I say under my breath.

Ping!

Grunt.

"Come. *On!*"

One last upward thrust and the surfboard breaks, but the nail pops out of the windowsill at the same time. It takes another few seconds to quietly jimmy the window open. Then I channel my inner zombie apocalypse cowgirl warrior and reach for the opening.

On a normal night, I would never leave the house after dark like this.

But this is not a normal night.

I roll ungracefully over the bottom of the window frame and freeze for a moment after I land. The sound of leaves and twigs crunching under my feet hits like a rockslide in my ears, and now I'm worried that it was loud enough for Gladys or Jordan to hear it too. I hold my breath for a few seconds, until it's for sure that no one's coming. Then I zigzag through the trees and stumps and freshly cut logs, slipping a few times as I lose traction on some clumps of leaves and grass, stumbling against broken twigs and rocks sticking partway out of the ground. I can finally see Mr. Noble's car parked on the corner, one good sprint ahead of me. I'm just about there, ready to reach out and open the back door, when a pair of headlights comes around the corner from behind us.

It's Renée. She must have gotten off work late.

I duck down fast, but Gentry sticks his head out the open window.

"*Ash*," he calls out.

"Shh." I hold my finger to my mouth, point at the truck going by. For a long minute, all I can hear is the sound of Renée's tires crunching over the gravel driveway, and the sound of blood rushing in my ears. She skids to a stop in front of the house. Opens and closes the truck door. Opens and closes the front door.

The front porch light goes off.

I jump into the back seat of Gentry's car and slump down as low as I can get.

"Can we go now?" I pant. "*Please?*"

Sam Noble
Wants to Know...

... **if he just helped me** run away from my foster home.

He doesn't say it in those exact words, but it's still what he means. I can't blame him for asking.

"Gladys doesn't like me to talk about home stuff," I tell him. "She says it's private."

"I understand, Ash, but I do know things aren't always easy there and . . . I just don't want to lose the opportunity for you to come over by breaking any rules, y'know?"

"You probably wouldn't believe me if I told you," I say in a jumble of panicked words.

"Try me."

I swallow hard.

"I think Jordan wants to hurt me."

Gentry turns and looks at me over his shoulder. Sam's eyes bounce-reflect off the rearview mirror, then back to the road.

"Can you say a little more about that?" he asks.

"Gladys's son? Jordan. Him and his wife . . . um, stay there sometimes, and he . . . he fixes things for Gladys, and . . . I mean . . . he nailed my bedroom window shut. That's what took me so long to get out."

After a stretch of silence, Sam says, "Okay." The word comes out long and thin, like he's thinking about it. "Why . . . why would you have to go through the—"

"And earlier, Gladys told him he wasn't allowed to hurt me. Like she *knew* he would try and do something if she didn't tell him not to."

I can see the back of Sam's head nodding slowly.

"Anything else?" he says.

It all sounds cringe now, even to myself. Like I'm making it up. Or making it out to be more than what it is. Like I'm being all dramatic about it.

"No," I say.

I lean my head against the window, watching as the boba tea place and the Starbucks and Big Al's roll by.

"Well, I don't mind at all if you stay tonight," Sam says around Fifth, as we pass the hospital. "And we have spare toothbrushes, in case you weren't able to bring anything with you, and . . . I'm sure you can borrow a change of clothes from Gentry if need be. But we'll have to tell your caseworker something. I really think you're going to have to let her know what's going on at home."

This time, the word *home* sticks in my throat like a dry cracker.

"Are *you* going to tell her?" I ask.

He doesn't answer right away. The high school whips in and out of view, then the old Civil War–era mansion that we took a field trip to last year.

"I'm not sure," he finally says as we pass Children's Park.

I nod. Swallow tears.

"Ash?" he says. "Do they . . . did they . . . have they ever hurt you?"

I blink fast. Blink faster. I'm not sure what he means by *hurt*. When Gladys complains about how expensive it is for things like food or clothes for me? When Jordan acts like everything bad that happens is my fault? When Gladys lets him call me things like baby-dyke . . . and worse? You can't show someone what that kind of hurt looks like, because it lives inside you instead of on your skin.

"What I'm asking is . . . have they ever physically put hands on you?"

I blink again, and one of my tears escapes down my cheek.

"Is that the only thing that will matter?" I ask. "If they hit me?"

"I doubt it, but . . . again, this is something to talk about with your caseworker."

"You can call her, but she won't answer," I say,

even though it's only partly true. "And she probably won't call back. She's always too busy."

"I'm going to have to talk to someone, Ash—"

"He's not even supposed to be in the house," I say, maybe a little louder than I need to. "No one is, except me and Gladys. But if I snitch about it . . ."

For a split second, I think about telling him what happened with the Manfredis, another foster family I had. That Mr. Manfredi, who I had to call Sergeant Manfredi, treated his home like it was boot camp and expected us to act like marines, even his own kids who weren't fosters. How one time, when my caseworker asked me how things were going and I told her about all the yelling and punishments, I got sent to live with the Fitches because of it. Mrs. Fitch made Sergeant Manfredi look like Captain Underpants.

"Look, here's what I know. I know we have to tell someone you're staying with us tonight, so . . . if you're being hurt, or there's an immediate threat to your safety, that will help me know how to go forward."

"What about the window . . . ?" I say.

He shakes his head. "Honestly, Ash, I'm not sure how it all works. I . . . We really just have to ask someone."

We turn left onto Ninth and wind through Chapmantown before pulling up in front of their house.

"So just to be clear...," Sam says. "No one has hit you?"

I shake my head.

There's no point in saying anything else. I've heard it a hundred times. There aren't enough caseworkers. There aren't enough foster families. There aren't enough resources to deal with a kid who *isn't* being hurt that way in the home.

And if that's just how it is... why even bother?

When We Wake Up...

...**my first thought is** whether Sam called my caseworker last night. I hold my breath as I fold up the blankets and sheets I slept on, waiting for him to say something about it.

In the kitchen, Sam has fresh waffles shaped like honeycombs coming off a bright-yellow waffle iron. He doesn't mention calling Barbara. I hope that means he didn't.

"I haven't done this in a minute," he says. "I used to make waffles all the time for Gentry's mom. Nothing she loved more than fresh waffles with blueberry syrup."

He says it like she's on a business trip somewhere, and she'll be home next Wednesday or something, and then he can make waffles for her again. He doesn't say it like she's gone forever. Or like his family tree got chopped to bits when she died. Or like their roots and branches can never be put back together again into something whole.

I look over at Gentry, but he's just standing there against the kitchen island, drinking orange juice, and I can't tell anything by his expression.

"Do you miss her?" I ask Sam.

"Oh yes." The sides of his eyes fold like little paper fans as he smiles. "I miss her every day. I miss her laugh—man, she had an awesome laugh. And she was *funny*. Right, Gentry?"

Gentry nods, but he still doesn't say anything, just stands there, eating and drinking and wiping syrup off his mouth with a napkin that looks like an old dish towel.

"Is it hard for you to make waffles?" I ask. "I mean . . . because they were her favorite, and now she's . . . gone."

Sam looks at me, but I feel like he probably only sees her.

"No," he says. "It's not hard at all. It's what keeps her alive. Telling our favorite stories about her. Making her favorite things sometimes. If we avoid talking about someone we've lost—that's when we lose them forever."

I nod. Take a bite of waffle. Chew slowly.

"My mom used to brush my hair when I was little," I finally say. "I remember sitting on her lap every morning, and . . . she grew my hair really long so she could brush it out and put it in these fancy braids and stuff. She said it was her favorite thing ever." It was mine too. Not having cutesy girl styles, but just . . . being close to her while she did my hair. Those were the moments I felt safest, even though I don't say that part out loud. "But . . . now those memories are mostly just . . . fuzz. Like I can barely remember what she looks like. Or how her voice sounds. I thought it was because I haven't seen her in so long, but . . ."

Sam stops eating to look at me.

"But what, Ash?"

"Do you think I'm forgetting because I don't see her anymore? Or because I stopped talking about her?"

"I don't know," he says. "How come you stopped?"

My fork shakes a little in my hand. I squint so I can figure out how to answer, so I can remember my whys. Did I want to stop visiting her, or did my foster families stop taking me? Either way, it doesn't explain why I never talk about her. Except that eight years is a long time to have a mom in jail. It may as well be forever to a four-year-old. It wouldn't have been forever, I mean—they actually let her out after she'd done the first half of her sentence. But she was back in jail a week later for doing the same thing she got arrested for in the first place. Only this time it was for longer. Once that happened, it seemed like no one wanted to talk about a kid's mom who's in jail, especially with that kid around. So maybe that's it. Maybe if everyone else stopped talking about her, mentioning her, letting me see her . . . wouldn't I do that too?

"I think . . . maybe because people don't want to hear sad things about a kid's life," I say as Sam takes a sip of coffee.

Gentry just keeps eating like everything about this conversation is normal, even though I've hardly ever talked about my mom or jail or any of that in front of him before. I never thought about telling anyone, least of all a grown-up, about those days. How my bedroom was off-limits because that's where she cooked meth. Or how a bunch of cop cars and fire trucks with lights and sirens all pulled up to our trailer at the same time. Or how they put her in handcuffs and took her away in one car and me in another. A four-year-old isn't supposed to remember those things. A twelve-year-old will try their hardest to forget.

"For what it's worth," Gentry's dad says, "I'd be happy to listen. Anytime."

He drops us off in front of the gym, waves as he drives away.

Gentry says nothing about my mom, or his mom, or his dad, or waffles. He acts like nothing's different about this morning.

For me, everything is different.

We head to homeroom, but the door's locked, so we sit on the ground outside it. He pulls a deck of Shattered! cards out of his backpack and shuffles them, and I still don't understand why Gentry's been so quiet this morning. Or how distant he seemed last night, setting out blankets on the couch for me to sleep on. I thought he was just tired, but now I'm not so sure.

"Are you mad at me?" I ask.

He doesn't answer. He flips over a rando card. It says *Demolished!* on it.

"Is it because I texted so late last night?" I ask.

"You wouldn't have texted if it wasn't important," he says, even though he hasn't even asked me about what happened.

He shuffles. Flips another card. *Busted*.

"So why are you mad?" I press.

He cuts me a look.

"I saw you walk off with Joss yesterday," he says.

Shuffle, shuffle, flip. Shuffle, shuffle, flip.

"Wait, you're mad because of *that*?"

He shoves the deck of cards back inside its black-and-red box.

"I know you like her," he says.

"I know *you* like her," I say back. "It's not even like that. I just want to be her friend. Can't I have another friend besides you?"

But he's out. Closed up tight like that box of Shattered! cards.

It doesn't matter what I say now. If I want to talk about what happened at Gladys's last night. Or why I asked his dad to come get me. Or what's going to happen when I go back. For me, that's all I can think about.

But it seems like even Gentry doesn't want to hear sad things about a kid.

Not even his BFF.

 ## Ms. Kim Tells Me...

. . . to stay after class a minute.

That can't be good.

I sit at my desk while everyone else leaves. Wiz and Matt try to see who can shove each other through the door first. Joss throws a look in my direction on her way out.

When it's just me and Ms. Kim in the room, she signals me to come forward. My free write is out on her desk. Man, I don't remember my answer being so short. And the picture I drew underneath it of a three-faced villainous Ms. Kim imposter looks like something I'm going to get in trouble for.

I lick my lips but try not to drop eye contact with her. That's hard to do with a teacher. But you can't let them see you sweat when they're trying to intimidate you.

"If I had to guess," she says, "I'd say you like drawing better than you like writing."

"That is correct," I say, secretly patting myself on the back for holding my chill.

She moves the paper a minuscule distance toward me, then pulls it back again.

"Well, you're not a bad writer," she says. "But."

I look down at the paper, brace myself. Here it comes.

"You're an *exceptional* artist."

I wait. When nothing bad happens, I glance up at her again, hoping I don't look like one of those big-eyed "surprise" emojis, even though that's what it feels like inside me.

Ms. Kim goes, "Can I ask you something?"

"... Okay."

"Can I ask about what you said? About your parents not coming to get you?"

I lick my lips again.

"It's not my parents," I tell her.

I expect a look of surprise to hit Ms. Kim's face, or a sound of some kind. Like *Oh*. Or *Gotcha*. But it doesn't.

"It's my foster mom, and she doesn't get paid to drive me around," I tell her, grabbing my cool back. "She gets paid to feed me and give me a place to sleep."

Ms. Kim nods. "Is that what she tells you?"

Now I'm feeling cringe all over again. The best way to handle a situation like this is to lock it all down. Don't answer. Don't nod. Just stare.

She breathes out through her nose, long and slow.

"I want you to know, Ash, I read your answers very carefully. I'll read everything you turn in very carefully. Even if you don't like writing assignments. Or sharing your personal thoughts and feelings."

She waits for me to respond. I don't want to. So I don't. I want to stay on lockdown. But lockdown goes on too long and now I just want to get out of there.

I just say, "Okay."

She nods again and I turn to leave.

"Oh, and Ash?"

My gut says *Don't do it*, but I turn around anyway.

"Very clever of you, turning Evil Ms. Kim into a nefarious three-headed imposter."

She smiles as she says this.

Maybe she's just glad I didn't reveal her as a true villain.

Or maybe . . . she really isn't a villain at all.

Mr. Mann...

...is out of control.

Now he's offering mega-bonus points if we go digital on our family tree project. He's like, "Think graphics! Think animation! Make magic!"

The thing is, even if I *wanted* to make magic, I still couldn't. Not everyone has computers at home. Or decent internet. Or a phone that can download apps.

Not everyone even wants to make a family tree in the first place.

Besides. It doesn't matter if I do make one—I'd still fail the project. It's never going to be what he wants, because I don't have three generations of a family to put on mine. Unless it counts as three generations to say: *Here's my mom. I don't have a grandma because her mom died when she was my age, so she got sent to foster care, got pregnant at seventeen, didn't know how to take care of me, made meth, sold meth, got put in jail for it, got out, sold more meth, and now she's in prison.* Or I guess I could do

"Three Generations: The Foster Care Edition": *This is my foster mom, Gladys, her son Jordan, his fake wife Renée, and their baby. But they're not supposed to live with us, so just pretend I never said anything about them.* I could cheat and put the Silvas as my family, since they actually wanted to adopt eight-year-old me. But that dream went *poof!* a year and a half later when Ana ended up having her twins. Her boy and girl. Her perfect family. *I'm so sorry, sweetheart*, they'd said, over and over until my caseworker came and got me. I know you're supposed to accept an apology, but I still can't. *I'm sorry* is for things like *We couldn't get tickets to the baseball game.* Not for when you're told your dreams of being part of a real family just got smashed to bits.

Joss slides in next to me.

"How's your project going?" she asks.

"How's yours?"

"I asked you first."

I know you like her.

I twist in my seat a little, sniff on the stealth to see if I smell bad, since my clothes are going on their second day.

"Yeah, I'm probably not gonna do it." I give her an I-don't-even-care shrug to show how much I don't even care. Then I do one more undercover sniff.

"Really?" she says. "Why not?"

"Because it sucks. Why—are *you* doing it?"

"Uh, yes, duh."

Joss pushes some of her hair behind her ear.

She goes, "You know . . . you can put whoever you want on it. Make stuff up. Make up a family. He'll never know if it's your *real* family or not."

I stare at her, wishing for once I could figure her out.

"Is that what *you're* doing?" I ask.

"Yup." She shakes her hair so it's not behind her ear anymore, twists it up, then lets it go. "Beats getting an F," she adds.

"Can I see it?"

That's when Joss starts closing off, like the trick wall of interconnecting bricks I created to hide the entrance to Drago's lair.

"Maybe. One day," she says. "When you're old enough to handle it."

I think she's joking.

But I also think she's not joking.

The vibe fizzles, and I scramble for something awesome to say. Or at least something that isn't not-awesome. I want to tell her how I used her zombie apocalypse–cowgirl skills to escape from Jordan last night. But if I did, then I'd have to get into the whole *I'm in foster care* thing, and I don't want to tell her about that—not yet. It was hard enough to tell Gentry the first time he invited me to his house last year, and I wouldn't have said anything even then, except his dad had to fill out some forms with Children's Services first. But Gentry was totally chill about the whole thing. "Well, it's just me and my dad," he'd said. "So you can be part of our family whenever you come over." Yeah, Gentry was great about it. But sometimes it changes how people think about you, so it's usually just easier not to say anything at all.

"What are you doing for lunch?" she asks.

My mind goes to Gentry again. To what he said this morning. How hurt he sounded, thinking I was trying to move in on his crush. I don't want him to think that, because it isn't true.

"I don't know," I say.

"Come sit with us," she says.

"With you?"

"Yeah."

"And your friends-not-friends?"

She laughs a little. "Yeah."

I stare down at the blank sheet of paper in front of me. The page that's supposed to have my complete rough draft on it. I can tell I'm making a face, but I can't unmake it now—she's already seen it.

"Come on," she says. "They're not that bad."

"Why? Because they don't beat you up?"

The smile melts right off her face.

"That's what you said, though, right?" I ask. "That you sit with those girls at lunch so they won't beat you up?"

Her mouth pops open.

"Why do you always do that?" she says.

"Always do *what*?" I ask, because I've barely known her a week—how could she know if I *always* do anything?

"Why do you always put up a wall like that, when people are just trying to be nice to you?"

We sit there blinking at each other like a game of chicken, like we both think the other person's being stubborn.

"You know what, Ash? Fine," she says. "Don't sit with us. I mean . . . God. Who hurt you?"

I blink at her as she walks away.

It's weird to see yourself how someone else sees you.

But also, someone else can only see what you show them. So why is it so hard to show people who we really are?

God. Who hurt you?

This time, my blink lasts a little longer. I know *who hurt you* is a thing people say to be funny. *Why would you put ketchup on your eggs—who hurt you?* And I know Joss can't know that literally everyone in my life has hurt me. Literally. Everyone. Even the Silvas.

Especially the Silvas.

And if she really wants to dig down to it, that's probably why I am the way I am.

1 When the Bell Rings for Lunch...

...I shove all my stuff into my backpack and peel out of class before everyone else. Before Joss.

I head straight for the cafeteria. No one gets to tell me where I can or can't eat. Only I can decide that. Just me. Alone. Like always.

I thought Joss was going to be a friend, but I was wrong. People suck.

Don't go into the cafeteria today—they're planning something.

I only sit with those girls so they don't beat me up.

The one thing I've learned so far in middle school is that if you don't look out for yourself, no one else will. Not in class. Not in the cafeteria. Not anywhere.

I get my lunch card out and go through the line. Orange slices. Nachos. Milk. No one's eating this food today but me. In the cafeteria. By myself. No matter who else shows up.

The lady swipes my card and hands it back, and

I squeeze it between two fingers as I carry my tray toward the tables. If I don't look around, I won't have to see Joss or Gentry or Wiz and them, even if they're here. Just like my alter ego Drago, I close my mental iris around everything else but an open spot at a table. That's all I need right now.

I find something better than an open spot. I find a whole empty table. But as soon as I sit down, someone reaches from behind me and slips the lunch card from between my fingers. I drop the tray onto the table and swing around.

"Give it back!" I snap.

Matt Adams holds it up away from me, too high for me to reach.

"I said *give it*!"

"Or what?" He sneers. "You'll sic your rainbow unicorn on me?"

I swipe for it, but he just laughs and waves it at me.

"You want this? You want it back? Beg for it, Ashley. *Beg!*"

Before he can tell me to beg for my card back one more time, he shouts "*Hey!*" and whips around.

We're both surprised to see Joss standing behind him, holding the card over her head. She must have snuck up on Matt and snatched it away from him somehow. I didn't even see her—that's how stealth she was.

She slides my lunch card into her back pocket and pushes right in between me and Matt.

"Get your tray," she tells me in a voice that's quiet but strong.

It takes me a second to shake out of my confusion and pick my tray up. Then she hooks her arm through mine and we head over to her table.

"This is Ash," she says to the other girls sitting there.

A few of them go, "Hey, Ash," as I sit down.

I'm still pretty disoriented, so I don't say anything, not even when Joss hands my card back to me.

She and her friends-not-friends are already done eating, so they just keep talking as I open my cheese packet and squeeze the nacho sauce over the pile of tortilla chips I emptied into the paper boat.

As disgusting as they are, these are the best nachos I've ever had in my whole life. They taste like victory.

Her friends-not-friends leave just before the bell rings.

Joss starts to get up, too, but I go, "Hey," and she flips back around to look at me.

"Why'd you do that?" I ask.

"You mean with Matt?"

"Yeah."

"He was being a jerk."

She starts to walk away, but I still don't move, so she swishes her hair over her shoulders as she turns back around.

"I couldn't just leave you there," she says. "A girl doesn't do that to another girl."

I nod. Maybe even smile, sort of.

"Come on." Joss takes my tray for me. "I'll walk to math with you."

 # "Do You Think...

"...we'll have a sub again for PE?" I ask.

"I hope not," Joss says. "I couldn't stand Mrs. Paul yesterday. Anyway. I like Mr. Carter. He's pretty cool, for a dude."

"Coach Miller too. I mean . . . she's not a dude, but . . ."

She snorts. "You're so funny, Ash."

I'm not sure what I said that was funny, but okay.

"So, where was G today?" she asks.

The question feels like a cloud crossing in front of the sun.

"I don't know," I tell her.

"Oh. I just figured . . . because you two seem kind of . . . attached."

I cut a quick look at her.

"Do you like him?" I ask.

She doesn't answer right off, just keeps walking, waves of brown hair with almost-blond tips curling behind her as we hit the breezeway.

"He sucks at *Mario Kart*," she finally says.

I blink at the ground a few times. "So, you like him."

"I don't know. I mean, guys are a pain in the butt."

"Yeah, I guess."

We turn toward the 100 wing where our math class is and sit down next to the closed door.

I go, "I think Gentry's probably okay, though. For a guy."

The words knock bruises into my chest on their way out. Gentry *is* okay. He's my best friend. And Joss could possibly even be a friend. And I'd rather have friends than a crush, anyway, because who else is going to be there when things get hard?

Mrs. Duncan opens the door. She looks down at us like she wasn't expecting to see anyone there, then motions for us to come in. I'm not ready to go inside, but Joss grabs my hoodie by the shoulder and pulls me up as she scrambles to her feet.

"Don't," I say. "You're gonna stretch it."

She rolls her eyes and lets go, but the spot where her fingers touched my shoulder still hums in surprise. I'm not used to being touched, not even in a friendly way.

I don't need to *like* like Joss.

Gentry likes Joss.

And Joss likes Gentry.

And I don't want Gentry to think I'm the kind of friend who would get in the middle of that. He's like my brother, which is a weird and cool thought to have.

I need to get back to him not having hurt feelings because of me, and . . .

Why does everything have to be so complicated all the time?

○ ◑ ○

"You're here early, Ash," Coach Miller says when I wander into the gym sixth period before anyone else does.

I skip the part about how I put my PE clothes on under my jeans and hoodie during break today. How I just slipped the jeans and hoodie off in the girls' room right after fifth and put them in my backpack so I wouldn't need to go into the locker room.

"Where were you yesterday?" I ask her.

"I had to take my dad to a doctor's appointment in Sacramento," she says, bending down to retie her shoelaces.

I try to imagine what Coach Miller's dad would look like, but all I can see is the old guy from the movie *Up*.

"How come he couldn't take himself?" I ask.

"He doesn't drive anymore," she says. "He has dementia, so my sister and I trade off when he needs something."

"Like driving to a doctor's appointment?"

"Exactly." She straightens up, and for the first time I notice how tall she is.

"What about your mom?" I ask.

Coach's smile looks sad.

"We lost my mom a couple of years ago, so it's just my dad, my sister, and me."

Man. Her dad really *is* the old guy from *Up*.

"I'm sorry that happened," I whisper.

"Thanks." She starts taking equipment out of a utility wagon. "How'd things go with the sub yesterday?"

"She was weird."

Her eyebrows shoot up like they're about to make a free throw.

"Weird how?"

"She told us we had to jump the wall so we could be prepared in case there's a zombie apocalypse."

Coach smiles. "That's different," she says.

I *could* tell her about climbing out of the window at Gladys's last night. She's standing barely three feet away, taking equipment out of a wagon. It wouldn't even be that strange, since we were just talking about how we jumped the wall to escape pretend zombies yesterday. I could tell her how much I don't like living there, especially since Gladys is breaking like a hundred rules by letting Jordan stay with us. Or about how Jordan's the literal worst. I mean . . .

I *could* tell her . . .

Taryn Swisher and her crew come bouncing into the gym. Squealing girls and squeaking shoes take over every inch of floor-to-ceiling space.

I guess it doesn't matter about Gladys or Jordan

or the zombie apocalypse. Coach Miller has enough things to think about. How her dad has dementia and can't drive. How she doesn't have a mom anymore. It might make her feel better to know that I understand about not having a mom around. Sometimes when two people have something like that in common, they can help each other get through it.

But she's taking equipment out of that wagon and telling the girls coming in where to line up and everything, and . . .

I just think she has too many sad things on her mind to tell her about my sad things.

No one wants to hear about a mom who's in prison.

Or that I used yesterday's fake zombie lesson to make a real escape last night.

Or that I don't feel safe at Gladys's, and I don't know what to do about it.

I watch her unpack that wagon and don't say anything at all.

When the Last Bell Rings...

... I'm not sure what to do.

I walk in the direction of the blacktop. Zombie walls to the left. Cemetery to the right. Gladys's straight ahead two miles. Gentry somewhere behind me, probably at ACE. Probably playing Shattered!, since that's so important to him.

I wish I could go sit in my tree and draw right now.

I look up from where I'm walking, and for the first time, I notice how the cemetery is full of trees. Big ones. Big and tall, with tons of branches and leaves still on them. A person could really hide in one of those trees. Get lost, maybe even.

I hurry in that direction.

The cemetery trees are a lot bigger than my walnut tree at Gladys's, which is both good and bad. I pick one with branches low enough to get a foothold, but not too high that I'd die if I fell out of it. Then I swing my bag around behind me and start climbing.

Once I'm up where I want to be, I take out my sketchbook and pencil, and flip to the last page I drew. It was from the day I got in trouble for not doing Ms. Kim's free write. Drago was about to vanquish three-headed Ms. Kim for cruel and unusual writing assignments. I flip to the page before that—the Joss Cruz page. Joss dropping pepperoni slices into her mouth in the cafeteria. Joss burning air out at the skate park. I only drew seven panels—I never got to finish the last one. I blink through images of her like camera clicks in my mind, trying to think of what to draw last. But I keep coming back to the same thing.

Joss and Gentry playing *Mario Kart*.

I draw them from the back, the way I watched them on Saturday. Leaning to the left as they drifted. A plate of random snacks on the table nearby.

As I add cookies and pretzels to the plate, I hear the *click-click* of someone riding a skateboard below me, and I know before I even see her that it's Joss. I almost call out, but I decide to watch her instead. "You're a keen observer," the traveling visual arts teacher told me last year. "That's what makes a good artist."

It isn't long before Joss rolls out of view. I lean forward so I can track her, but it's only another click or two before I can't see her again. I lean a little more. A little more.

There. She's stopped. At a headstone. I study the

paths between here and there so I can figure out later which one it is. Joss kicks her board out from under her and kneels down in front of the headstone, crossing herself as she does. I can't hear if she's saying anything. Or if she's crying. She's too far away, so all I can do is watch. And wonder. What does it feel like to have a grandma you knew once, and loved, and lost? I had to leave the Silvas before the grandparents ever came to visit, so I only just heard about them and saw a few pictures. Now I'm afraid I'll never have that chance again. I can only see what it looks like for someone else, from too far away to really get the whole picture of it.

After a while, Joss stands up again, scoots her deck out in front of her, and hops on.

A couple of blinks later, she's gone.

I'm kind of sorry I drew the *Mario Kart* picture now. I wish I would have drawn Joss at her grandma's grave instead. Maybe I'll make that a whole separate picture. Maybe I'll give it to Joss as a thank-you for helping me at lunch today.

Or . . . I don't know. Maybe not. I don't usually show my art to people—too risky. They'll probably just make fun of it. I learned that lesson when I was with the Fitches, too, as if their jerky kids could have done any better.

When I'm done sketching out the basic lines of my new picture idea, I pack my stuff up and climb back down, trying to remember where Joss's grandma's headstone is. Lucky for me, it's not too hard to find.

I stay off to one side as I look at it, mostly out of respect. I mean, she's not *my* grandma. Plus, it seems kind of rude to stand right on top of where someone's buried.

The engraved words on the shiny, flat stone say: *Amelia Cruz—Madre, Abuelita, Alma Y Corazón De La Familia.* Underneath that it says: *Que Descanse En Los Brazos De Su Dios.*

I don't know what those Spanish words all mean, but I feel something radiating from them, something bigger than the words themselves. Like an energy, if that doesn't sound too weird.

I sit down cross-legged on the dirt and leaves and pull my sketchbook out. When I lean in to draw the headstone, I notice the dates that show Amelia Cruz's birth and death. She only just died a few months ago, right before summer started. The way Joss talked about losing her grandma . . . for some reason I felt like it was something that happened a long time ago. I had no idea how fresh that all was for her. Her grandma must have died right around the time they moved here. I wonder if that's why they came. So they could be with her awhile before she died.

I copy the words carefully so I don't get them wrong. How is it possible that I can feel love coming out of a cold piece of stone, from words carved into it that I don't even understand, about a person I never knew? How can I feel that, but I don't feel anything remotely like that from the people I live with, who are supposed to care about me?

I blink the sting of that thought away, because it doesn't really matter. It's just facts.

I want you to know, Ash, I read your answers very carefully.

Grown-ups always want you to think they care about what happens to you. Maybe they mean it when they say it. But everyone has their own lives. And their own families. Everyone gets too busy to notice that things are bad sometimes.

Until it's too late.

It's Pretty Late...

...when I turn off the Esplanade and onto Eleventh. Way later than it usually is when I get home. Except I don't consider this house as my home. And I really wish I didn't have to go back there tonight.

But where else can I go? Nowhere.

I'm just a few steps past the little store on the corner of Eleventh when Renée's truck drives by, then zips to the side of the road like she's waiting for me.

"Hop in, Ash," she says, pushing the door open when I get there.

She seems kind of out of breath.

"Why are you off work so early?"

"Oh," she says, dragging the word out like she's trying to think up a reason. "I had to run some errands. For Jordan's birthday coming up."

I look at her on the stealth so she can't see the way I don't believe her.

"Okay," I say.

"And if anyone asks," she says, her eyes almost

closing, like the metal iris leading into Drago's lair, "you were helping me. Okay?"

She finally looks at me and I look at her.

"Sure," I say, real quiet.

Renée pulls back onto the road, goes down to the next street, turns right, then right again.

Jordan is out in the yard when we pull up, hacking away at one of the trees he and Kenny chainsawed the other day, chopping it into cordwood. I sneak another look at Renée. She wipes her upper lip with the side of her hand and takes a deep breath before getting out of the truck.

Jordan sinks his axe into the stump base as we walk up.

"Where the hell have you been?" he says.

But he's looking straight at me, not at Renée.

"I . . . uh . . ."

"Don't be mad at Ash. I asked her to help me run some errands. Right, Ash?"

"Um . . ."

"What kind of errands?" He grabs the axe handle and wiggles it back and forth a few times, like a reminder. Like a threat.

"Anyone with a birthday coming up probably shouldn't ask too many questions," Renée says with a fake smile.

"Well, you just have an answer for everything, don't you?" he says in mocking voice.

The air goes still and quiet for a few seconds.

Even the birds and the leaves on the trees seem like they're holding their breath. He pulls that axe out of the stump—now he's just standing there, holding it like Paul Bunyan or something.

"What about this morning?" He spits the question at me like he already knows the answer. Like he's just waiting to catch me in a lie so he can punish me. "Where were you?"

I look at the freshly cut tree stump. Then at the axe in his hands.

You can't touch that kid, Gladys had said to him. I wonder if he still listens to his mother.

"I already told you," Renée says. "Ash got picked up early for school."

"By who?"

She takes a breath to tell him, but he holds a finger up right in front of her face and says, "*Let her answer.*"

She still looks like she wants to say something, but she forces herself not to.

"My friend's dad," I whisper, looking at the ground the way Gladys's dog Frampton did whenever Jordan yelled at him.

"Which friend?"

A siren wails down the Esplanade toward the hospital. I wait till the sound fades before saying, "Gentry."

"*Gentry?* What kind of name is that?"

What kind of question is that?

Renée steps forward. "Jordan—"

"Sounds kinda *gay* to me," he says, pushing her back.

I want to tell him how wrong it is to say that, but I can't. I can barely even catch my breath right now.

"So why was your window open this morning, Ash? Huh? How do you explain that?"

"It gets really hot in there," I say, keeping my voice quiet. "I just forgot to close it."

His eyes harden on me again, like he knows for sure I'm lying. I mean, the nail . . .

"Let's go inside," Renée tells him, taking him by the arm. "I brought some take-and-bake pizzas home. They were free—Dave had coupons for us in the break room."

Her voice trails off as she leads Jordan into the house. She throws a look over her shoulder at me just before the door closes.

I don't realize how scared I am until it comes out of me in hot breath and tears. Jordan gets mad when people have emotions, especially when they cry. And he's already mad, so I know I have to stop. But I can't. And I can't go inside until I do.

I wipe my eyes on my sleeve and turn away from the house, and that's when I see it.

The axe.

Not the one he was just holding, but the other one, the one Kenny was using yesterday.

It's right there. Sunk into the side of my tree.

Just . . . waiting.

 # He's Gonna Chop It Down.

My tree.

He already chopped down two other trees right next to mine, and now my tree has an axe sticking out of it.

"Over my dead body," I whisper, kicking up gravel and debris as I race toward the front porch.

My sad tears turn to angry tears the closer I get. I'm hyperfocused, Drago at my back as I throw the door open. Jordan and Renée and Gladys are all standing there, frozen in midfight as I blast into the room.

"Why are you cutting all the trees down?" I shout.

Renée sticks her arm out like a human guardrail as I rush up to Jordan.

"Ash—" she says.

"They've got root rot or something," Gladys spits, thinking that'll shut me up.

"That's a lie! There's nothing wrong with those

trees! You just don't want me to have anything for myself!"

Suddenly the adults are all talking at once.

"Honey, stay out of this." "Shut up!" "Go to your room." "Let it go, Ash." "Just let it go." "*Let it go!*"

But I can't let it go.

I may not have a family tree, but I have *this* tree, and it's all I have, and it's mine, and now Jordan wants to take it from me.

I pounce toward him with my fists swinging.

Everyone. Always. Wants. To. Take. Everything. Away. From. Me.

"You can't have it!" I shout, swiping at him. "It's mine! You can't take it!"

The word "Stop!" sounds different coming out of each of their mouths, but I don't stop. I can't.

Not until Jordan finally screams:

"Get her under control!"

All the commotion freezes for a moment before falling to the ground in a billion pieces of shattered air. Gladys wraps her fingers around one of my arms and Renée puts a hand on my shoulder, but no one moves after that, not even Jordan.

It's so quiet, I can hear everyone's breath. Renée's is extra fast, and Jordan's is extra hard. Gladys sounds wheezy like always. And I'm holding mine.

The gas in the oven clicks like it does when it's heating up.

Marcus starts crying from his room. Our room.

The room Jordan nailed the window shut in so I could never escape.

Jordan says a swear word before flying out the front door. It only takes a second to realize what he's doing, and when I do . . .

I scream.

And scream.

At the sound of the chainsaw.

At the nonstop buzz-and-grind of its gnashing teeth.

I scream the same word, over and over again.

"No!"

Renée tells Gladys, "I've got her," and Gladys lets me go as Renée wraps both her arms around me, tight enough to hold me but not too tight for me to breathe. She tries to calm me down, whispering in my ear.

"It's okay, honey. It'll be fine, I promise. It's okay."

But it's not. I know Jordan hits Renée. How can I believe her when she tells me it'll be fine? It's never fine. Not even for her.

The sound of the chainsaw cuts through the tight air all around us. Renée hasn't let me go yet, and I fight to get away from her until I hear my tree crash to the ground.

Jordan comes back inside, all thick breath and sweat.

"Make sure I don't see her again tonight," he says, pointing a sharp finger at me.

Renée takes me to my room. The door clicks shut behind her.

After she leaves, I look around, the way I did on my very first day with Gladys, when she lived in the trailer up in Oroville. The trailer was small, but it was nice—nicer than this house. Gladys showed me the room that was still mostly a knitting-and-sewing room, but with a bed and a dresser she said I could use. She told me to get settled, but I honestly never felt settled there. Because it never felt like home, especially after leaving the Silvas. Being torn from the Silvas and shoved in front of Gladys's unhappy face . . . and as quick as it all happened . . . that didn't feel safe. It felt like when I'd sit on a bench at the transit station while my mom bought our monthly bus pass. Those times always seemed a little scary. I didn't know what kinds of people would show up or if there was going to be a fight. All kinds of ugly stuff used to happen at the transit station. And the worst part was, I knew we'd have to come back again next month.

That's how I imagine prison is for my mom too. Like sitting at the transit station with different people constantly coming and going, doing ugly things, making her scared or nervous. Making her fight just to protect herself. Because that's how she always survived after her mother died. "Don't you touch me!" she'd scream at a man on the bus, or a man in the liquor store, or the woman who called the police on us at the ice cream shop, who told my mom, "You shouldn't be wasting money on ice cream, if you're so poor." My mom said, "Don't tell me how to raise my kid." And when that lady and her kid squeezed right in front of us anyway, my mom went, "Hey! My kid deserves ice cream just as much as your kid does!" and shoved her out of the line. The cops let her off with a warning that time, but I think that's the kind of thing that happens to her a lot. Even in lockup. "I don't have mean bones," she told me once when I visited her, just before they transferred her to prison. "I just have a heart for survival. Remember that, Ash. You're gonna need it."

Marcus whimpers in his Pack 'n Play. I hand him the plushie he threw onto the floor. Then I turn toward the window.

Instead of a nail, there's a screw now. I know it's a screw because it has that little plus sign on the top. It's a lot harder to pull out a screw than a nail, but I'm sure Jordan is aware of that. I know he knows I snuck out, and that's why he put it there. I wonder if Gladys realizes he did it.

After a while, there's a soft knock on my door, and Renée comes in before I can say for her to. She's holding a paper towel folded around a slice of pizza.

"I came to get Marcus," she whispers.

"Okay."

She sets the paper towel on top of the dresser, then goes to pick the baby up. She gets his diaper bag, too, like she's planning on going somewhere. I kinda wish she'd run away with him, but I also kinda hope she doesn't. Sometimes Renée seems like the best part of living here—mostly on her days off, since she's not home very much. If she did run away, I could maybe go with her. Because if it wasn't for Jordan, she'd probably be an okay mom.

Before she opens the door to leave, she turns around to look at me.

"Everything is going to be okay, Ash. I promise."

"Okay."

"But . . . um . . . please don't mention the pizza to Jordan."

She stares at me, right in my eyes, the way Drago does when she's trying to communicate telepathically.

I nod back.

But everything is not okay.

And she's not someone I can believe in anymore.

 *I Have to Pee...*

...really, really bad. But I decide to wait until everyone's loud, angry talking quiets down, and then their still-angry-but-less-loud talking. I'll wait even longer if I have to—until the sun goes all the way down and everyone's asleep. Or at least when Gladys finally stops making threats to Jordan, and he and Renée are in their own room with the door closed. I'll wait until it feels safe enough to walk down the short hallway, since we only have one bathroom and it's right next to them.

Until then, all I can do is sit here with my Discman on, volume up high, and look out the window at the stump where my tree used to be. And cry. Jordan can be mad about me crying all he wants. I don't even care anymore.

When it's too dark to see my tree stump outside, I start loading up my backpack with everything I could ever need to run away and not come back. My sketchbook and pencils. All my socks and underwear—which isn't that much, honestly—rolled into a ziplock baggie that smells like baby wipes. A few shirts and pants. My school stuff, obviously. My phone is on the charger, just to be sure. I put my PE clothes on under the clothes I'm wearing, like I did before.

By the time I zip my backpack closed, I decide I can't hold it in any longer. I tiptoe to the door and put my hand on the knob.

The blast of a scream stops me.

It's Renée.

"No! I said, keep your hands off me!"

I close my eyes, hear my mom say *Don't you touch me!* to one of a billion creepy dudes.

"I'll put my hands wherever I want!" Jordan screams back.

"Don't touch me, Jordan, or so help me God—"

"So help you God, what? *What*, Renée, you'll call the cops? You think they'll even come out here? They're *sick* of you calling 'em by now."

I turn. Look at my phone plugged into the wall. Look back at the door.

My hand is shaking hard as I pick up the phone. If I call them, he can't get mad at Renée for it. But he can get mad at me if he figures out I did it, and I don't know what would happen then. Not even Gladys has been able to stop his rages lately.

I put it back down.

Jordan is screaming ugly, horrible things at Renée.

Gladys is shouting at them from the living room to shut up.

"You're gonna wake the baby!" she barks.

Marcus instantly starts crying that high-pitched baby cry, and Gladys goes, "See? What'd I tell ya!"

Poor Marcus. He doesn't deserve any of this. He never asked to be born into this family. Who would choose to have Jordan for a dad?

I grab the phone.

If I'm too chicken to do it for myself, or even Renée, I could at least call for Marcus. Someone probably should have called to get help for me, way before my bedroom blew up.

The fight rages on the other side of the door. It spills out of their room and down the hallway. It sounds so loud and close, it almost seems like they're right next to me.

I dial 911.

When the lady on the other end of the phone asks me what my emergency is, I don't say anything, just hold the phone up so she can hear the fighting.

"Can I get your name?" she says. "Hello? Are you okay? Are you in any danger?"

I don't answer. If I don't say anything, I never have to admit I was the one who called. Maybe Jordan will think it was a neighbor or something. The cops will still know where to go if I keep quiet—at least that's how it works on TV. Those cop shows Gladys likes to watch, they always know where someone's calling from, even if that person never says anything.

Either it works, or a neighbor hears the fighting and calls 911 as well.

Because a few minutes later, red-and-blue flashing lights stop on the gravel driveway.

I peek through the flimsy blinds. Two police officers, a man and a woman, get out of the car and walk up to the house. I back away from the window, slink to the floor, make myself as small as possible so I can fit between the bed and the wall again. That way, no one will see me if they come in.

I hear the front door open.

Gladys says, in a voice like everything is perfectly fine, "What can I do for you?"

"We're here to do a welfare check," the man's voice says.

"Oh? On who?"

"Cute baby," the woman says. "Is he yours?"

Gladys grunts, like she's shifting Marcus from one hip to the other.

"This is my grandson, yes. I'm watching him tonight."

"Where are his parents?" the woman asks.

"I'm his father." Jordan's voice slips past my door into the living room.

The woman cop makes baby talk with Marcus, probably because he's upset and crying, while the man asks Jordan what his name is. I'm a little surprised he doesn't lie about it.

"Where's the baby's mom?" the man asks.

Gladys starts to answer, but Jordan talks right over her.

"Oh, she's sleeping," he says, all polite-like.

"Can you wake her up, please?"

There's a long, itchy silence at the end of this question, until Jordan finally asks, "What's this about, anyway?"

The woman says, "Sir, either you can wake her up, or I will. It would be much better on my report if you did it."

My heart is beating hard and fast as Jordan's footsteps pass by my room again on the way to his. I hear him whisper something to Renée, but I can't tell what. Then I hear them shuffle back toward the living room.

"Good evening, officers," Renée mumbles.

"Good evening," the woman says. "Can I get your name?"

"Renée. Banks."

"Renée, I'm Officer Brown and this is Officer Reed. Can I talk to you outside for a minute?" she asks.

"Look," Jordan says. "My wife is exhausted. It's been a long day. Our place has a gas leak and we had to find somewhere to stay for a few nights, so we're here with my mother. Can't you just let her—"

"It'll only take a moment. Officer Reed will be happy to stay here with you."

The front door squeaks open, then shut. Footsteps crunch the gravel and dried grass and the billions of twigs and bark chunks that came off the trees Jordan chopped down, and when the crunching stops, Renée and Officer Brown are right outside my window.

"Renée, did you call 911 tonight?"

"No," she says. "I didn't. I swear."

"Is there anyone else in the house who might have?"

I hold my breath. Part of me prays she won't mention me. But another part of me wishes she would.

"Mm—not that . . . not that I can think of, no."

"Take a moment," Officer Brown says. "Take all the time you need to think about it."

I want to peek through the blinds to see what's going on, but as soon as I imagine getting up, a new fear sneaks into my bones. The fear that after the police leave, Jordan's going to come smashing into my room and take everything that just happened out on me. Because if Renée doesn't lie and tell Officer Brown she called them, Jordan will know I did it.

"Sometimes my mother-in-law lets the baby play with her phone," Renée says. "Maybe that's what happened?"

"And there's no one else here?"

"No, ma'am."

"Renée, do you feel you're in any danger tonight?" Officer Brown asks.

She doesn't answer.

"I'm asking because, when you came out, it looked like you'd been crying. Do you feel safe? Is your baby safe?"

"Look, we have our problems like everyone else," Renée finally says. "But I'm handling things in my own way."

"Would it be helpful if you or your husband stayed somewhere else for the night?"

Yes! I want to jump up, pound on the screwed-shut window, and shout, *Take Jordan, take him somewhere else! Forever!*

"It's fine," Renée says instead of saying yes. "We're fine."

When they go back inside, I realize the other officer has been standing in the living room talking to Jordan, with only Gladys there to hear what he says. If he's lying to that cop, it's not like his mother's going to snitch about it.

"He thinks the call may have been made by a disgruntled neighbor," the cop tells his partner. "Some sort of dispute over noise."

"Yeah, they . . . they work graveyard," Jordan says. "Always sleeping during the day. Anyway, I was cutting down some of my mom's trees this week—guess they don't like the sound of the chainsaw waking 'em up all day."

What a liar.

There's a flurry of talking that I only catch parts

of. "Ah, that makes sense." "I wouldn't much like that either." "Maybe next time you could . . ." Mumble mumble mumble.

Officer Reed apologizes for the inconvenience.

Officer Brown thanks Renée for talking to her.

Then they get back into their police car and drive away into the night.

The first thing I hear after they're gone is a few heavy foot stomps that sound like they're coming straight toward my room.

"*Jordy*," Gladys whisper-screams. "Don't you touch that kid, or I'll call 'em back and tell 'em to take you away!"

I hold my breath, crouch even lower, push even harder against the wall.

"Get back in that room," he finally says to Renée, barking commands at her all the way down the hall, like she's Gladys's old dog Frampton. As the door shuts, he says, "You can start by telling me why you called the cops again."

I stay up all night, crammed into the only sliver of space that feels anything close to safe in this whole house, listening to him hurt her.

Listening to her cry.

Listening to Marcus cry.

And me, crying for them both.

In the Morning...

...**it seems like Gladys is** trying to make sure Jordan doesn't do anything bad to me before I have a chance to leave for school. She doesn't say that's what it is, but I can tell.

She even walks Marcus up and down the short hallway in front of the bathroom instead of around the living room like she usually does, while I finally take the longest pee of my life.

"Get your stuff," Gladys says, low and quiet, as I come out of the bathroom. "I'll drive you."

"Oh. That's okay. I can walk," I tell her, thinking about Marcus, how he cried most of the night and probably needs to be put down in his Pack 'n Play to sleep.

"I said, I'll take you. Now go get your stuff."

When I come back out with my fully loaded backpack, she looks at it for a beat or two but doesn't say anything. She just goes, "We'll stop at McDonald's for breakfast."

I'm not used to her being nice to me like this. She

was definitely nicer in the year or so before Jordan moved in. More relaxed, not as stressed all the time. But she's never taken me to McDonald's on the way to school before. And she doesn't usually act like she feels bad for me, even though she has tons of things to feel bad for.

But I just go, "Okay," and she pushes me out the door with Marcus wobbling on her hip.

When we go through the drive-through, Gladys gets me two Egg McMuffins because she thinks I didn't get any dinner last night. She doesn't know about the slice of pizza Renée snuck into my room when she came in to get Marcus, and I'm not going to say anything about it. I'm still grateful for the two Egg McMuffins, and not just because I'm starving, which I am. It's because that way I can give one to Gentry. So he knows I'm the kind of friend who shares her breakfast, not the kind who would steal his crush.

When Gladys drops me off in front of school, she asks, "Think you can spend the night with that Noble kid tonight, Ashley? Just to give Jordy some cooling-off time."

Why can't Jordan stay somewhere else? I think.

But all I say is "I'll figure it out."

"Let me know if you can't," she says. "I just think . . . y'know."

Yeah. I know.

I wave at her as she and Marcus drive off, but I don't think she sees me.

The McDonald's bag crinkles in my hand as I cross the grass toward the gym. I sit on the metal bench under the big Cougars sign, where me and Gentry always sit before school.

My stomach growls loud enough to hear *and* feel, so I open the bag and take out one of the Egg McMuffins. I go in for a huge bite, and just as I'm working through my chew, Gentry comes around the corner, this time in a vintage-looking Hawaiian shirt with the sleeves cut off.

He slows down some when he sees me.

"How'd you get here so early?" he asks.

"Gladys dropped me."

He looks skep.

"She bought me breakfast too. I got an extra one for you, if you want it."

I hold the bag out to him, and he sits next to me and takes it.

"Thanks," he mumbles as he unwraps the paper. "Why's she being so nice all of a sudden?"

I finish chewing and swallow before saying, "I . . . Cuz of something that happened last night, probably."

"Must have been bad," he says.

I nod and he nods and we keep eating, and then he notices my backpack busting at the seams.

"Dang, Ash. You got a body in there or something?"

I don't laugh, but I also don't not-laugh. It's one of those awkward half laughs.

"Is it Jordan?"

"Ha," I say, not-really-laughing again.

"So, what happened last ni—"

"I don't like Joss that way," I blurt.

He turns, squints at me. "What?"

I shake my head. "I would have told you if I did. I mean, I like her, just . . . as a friend."

"It didn't look that way the other day, though. Y'know?"

I nod. Look over at Gentry, who's looking over at me.

"I didn't know she'd be there," I say. "But she actually helped me with my panic attack."

"You were having a panic attack?"

I nod again.

"How come?"

"Things have just been . . . kinda hard," I say.

He looks down at his half-eaten McMuffin. "I'm sorry I was more upset about the thing with Joss than the thing with Jordan," he tells me.

"Thanks. We're good, though, right?"

He holds his fist out to me and I bump it. He explodes his at the end.

I finish the rest of my McMuffin in one bite, and so does he, and we sit there, watching people crisscross the lawn in front of us. Some of them shuffle across the grass like they're headed for the electric chair. A small group stops to toss a Frisbee around. Taryn Swisher walks by holding hands with some guy from my PE class.

"Just so you know," I add, "I think Joss likes you."

I'm not sure why I tell him that, except that it's probably true.

He flips in my direction.

"You do?"

"Yeah, I think so."

"Why—did she say something?"

"No."

"Then why do you think she likes me?"

"Because when I asked her, she *didn't* say anything."

He looks confused, but the bell rings before I can explain it to him. I finish on our way to homeroom.

"If she didn't like you, she would have gone *Ew! No! Gross!* But she didn't, so."

"Huh. I don't really get it. Is that a girl thing?"

I make a face and shrug. "I guess?"

"Okay."

By the time we get to homeroom, it feels like I can breathe a little easier with Gentry. But only until I think about last night. Then it's like I'm carrying an entire elephant around on my shoulders.

We slide into our seats, and just before the tardy bell rings, Gentry leans over and whispers, "I still want to know about what happened last night."

"Jordan got . . ." I don't know how to finish, so I just say, "Do you think I can stay over again?"

"Good morning!" Miss Moua says, cutting off any chance of Gentry answering as class gets started.

Right away, she puts us into small groups, then

hands us these little dice things with pictures instead of dots on the sides. She calls them story cubes. We're supposed to toss the dice and then make up a story from the pictures that come up.

When it's my turn, I just sit there looking at the pictures of a dog, a swimming pool, a chicken leg, and a snowman without saying anything. My cubes should have an axe, a tree stump, a cop, and someone hiding in the dark. That's a story I could tell, even if I didn't want to.

"Come. On," Kendalyn Meyer says, all irritated as I sit there staring at the dice. "Just make something up."

"It's not a big deal," Benjie Ross adds. "We all did it."

I push away from the desk, go over to where Miss Moua is.

"What's up, Ash?" she asks with an easy smile.

Nothing in my body feels easy right now.

"I can't concentrate on telling a story," I say.

"Did the baby keep you awake last night?" she asks.

"Um . . ." It would be so simple to say yes, but I'd feel bad about lying to her. So I just say, "Sort of."

She looks at me in a kind of way like she sees something. A way that makes me nervous.

"How can I support you?" she asks.

"Would you let me skip my turn just this once?"

"Of course."

"I promise I'll tell a story next time," I say.

Miss Moua's face goes serious. "Is there anything else I can do, Ash?"

But I just shake my head, because there are too many things. Too many things she *could* do, and nothing anyone *can* do.

In Science Class Second Period...

... Wiz Porter throws his backpack on the table and flops on top of it like he's about to take a nap. The reek of his body spray just about knocks me off my stool.

"You stink," I tell him.

"You stink worse," he says. "At least my Axe blocks your stench."

His words sting because they're probably true. But what really makes my stomach jump is the sound of the word *axe*.

Snapshots of yesterday click through my head.

Mr. Torres's voice bursts into the room as he tells us we're going to start an experiment today.

"We'll be using *charcoal* to purify *water*."

Mr. Torres sounds like he thinks he's talking to his potions class or something, and Wiz perks right up, nodding and saying "*Yes!*" like he's been waiting his whole life for this moment.

Some girl from my PE class calls out, "Is this for the zombie apocalypse?" and a few of the girls from PE laugh at that.

There's a few minutes of chaos while Mr. Torres tells us how to get our science experiments set up at our tables. Of course, Wiz offers to go get all the stuff we need. He thinks since he's a wizard, no one but him can figure anything out.

While he's gone, I try to sniff myself without anyone noticing. It's been a couple of days since I had a shower or changed my clothes.

For the first time, I kind of understand the whole body-spray thing, and for a split second, I wish I had some.

Wiz comes back with a tray full of cool chemistry stuff and sets it between us on the table. I spin on my stool a little and lean in to see what's there.

Wiz pitches back, waving his hand in front of his face. *My* face combusts like a science experiment gone sideways.

"What's your problem—" I start to ask, but before I can finish, he shoves his arm through a tiny unzipped opening in his backpack and comes out with a can of store-brand Axe. He pushes it at me, and I look around to make sure no one else is looking before hiding it inside my hoodie.

Then I stumble to the front of the class and ask Mr. Torres if I can go to the bathroom real quick. He waves me out.

Inside the bathroom stall, I spray myself down as fast as I can.

Wiz doesn't look at me when I come back into class, or when I sneak-return the fake Axe to him. He just unzips his backpack barely enough to slip it back inside.

By the end of class, we've created a setup that will allow us to filter out impurities and purify water in just a few days. Which is potentially kind of cool.

Now I just wish there was some kind of science experiment to help filter away all the impurities from my actual life.

Since we have third period together, too, Wiz ends up following me to English, not on purpose. He stays far enough behind me so that no one, probably including me, thinks we're walking to class together.

I notice Joss isn't there when the bell rings. I wonder if she's sick or something.

Meanwhile, Ms. Kim puts a writing prompt up on the board like she always does.

I wish I never had to . . .

I get what's going on here—I'm totally onto her. Ms. Kim gives us these writing prompts to trick us into sharing personal things about ourselves. *I'll read everything you turn in very carefully*, she'd said. *Very carefully.*

Let's see how carefully she really does read what I turn in:

> *I wish I never had to hide on the floor again*
> *while the cops come to the door*
> *and ask all these pointless questions:*
> *Who what why?*
> *When all anyone ever does is lie.*
> *I wish I never had to*
> *hear the cops say,*
> *"Sorry to bother you,*
> *sir and ma'am.*
> *Have a nice day."*
> *Then drive off into the night*
> *while the grown-ups*
> *keep fighting*
> *like feral cats and stray dogs.*
> *I wish I never had to go back there,*
> *back where Jordan cut down the perfect tree*
> *and now there's nowhere safe to go.*
> *But . . . writing a poem*
> *doesn't change things for me.*
> *And wishes can never*
> *grow back trees.*

After I write the last word, I try to swallow away the burn in my throat. I turn my paper over so no one has a chance to see it but the teacher. I can always tell her it was just a made-up poem, if she gets too weird about it.

Since my paper is already face down, I spend the rest of our free-write time doodling on the back of it. I doodle my screwed-shut window, only from the outside so I can keep that a secret. I doodle my tree in the yard that's just a stump now, with rings like scars pulsing across the flat top. I use dots instead of lines to draw in the ghost part of the tree, the part that isn't there anymore. I even add myself—well, just my legs, actually—made up of dots and dangling from my favorite limb. I doodle a speech bubble of Marcus crying from inside our room, and make it stretch all the way out the window. I *don't* doodle a huddled figure hiding on the floor next to the bed. She's there. But Ms. Kim doesn't need to know about that either.

The free write is almost over when the door opens, and Joss comes in. She doesn't look around, just keeps her eyes down as she hands her pass to Ms. Kim. It seems like she's upset, but I don't know her well enough to be sure.

When Ms. Kim calls time and tells us to pass our free writes up to her, I don't. I keep it folded up in my lap until the end of class and stay behind until everyone else is gone.

Then I drop it on her desk real fast and hurry out.

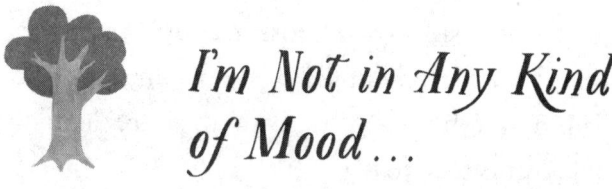# I'm Not in Any Kind of Mood...

. . . for Mr. Mann today.

Not for family tree talk.

Or teacher-splaining about dynasties and empires.

I'm not feeling any of it.

Especially not Steven Tyler and Chase Williams. They keep cutting up, and Mann never does anything to stop them. They keep looking over here, too, which probably means they made another humiliating meme about me or something.

I sneak a glance over at Joss—she still has her eyes glued to her feet. I sketch that image out real quick on my still-blank family tree paper.

Taryn Swisher walks by my desk on her way to the pencil sharpener.

She taps her freshly sharpened pencil on my desk on the way back. I don't know what her problem is. She's probably still bitter that I wouldn't draw her ginormous family tree for her, even though she's probably doing it in Google Slides now like everyone else, so it doesn't even matter.

The girl who sits next to Joss gets up to go sit by her friends on the other side of the room, and since Mr. Mann doesn't seem to care if we're actually working, I go sit by Joss.

"Why were you late today?" I whisper-ask.

She doesn't answer right off. The way she stares at the floor, I can't decide if she wishes it would open up and swallow her, or if she expects something to crash up through it from deep inside the earth.

"I got my period," she finally says. "I had to go to the nurse because I didn't have anything with me."

I look around the room, then back at Joss. "Once, I saw Bryan Fernández give a tampon to Jessa Whitley. He said he always keeps some in his backpack because he has six sisters and someone always needs one."

She finally looks at me.

"Cool," she says. It doesn't sound sarcastic, but I do feel like there's something else there, something hidden behind that single, soft word.

I decide to make a bold move.

I ask, "So . . . what else is going on?"

She looks away. "What makes you think something else is going on?"

"If I'm wrong, you can just say so."

But she doesn't tell me I'm wrong. She doesn't tell

me anything. She sits there with her arms crossed and her head down and her hair falling along the sides of her face.

"People suck," she finally says.

I wonder who she means by *people*. A boy? A teacher? A parent? *People* as an answer can be pretty open to interpretation.

"What are you doing for lunch?" I ask, wanting to say something helpful even though I don't always know how.

She shrugs, but only with one shoulder.

"You can hang out with me and Gentry," I offer. "Or we can sit with your friends—"

She snorts and goes, "I'm over the whole cafeteria thing."

Wow. That's a daring statement to make barely two weeks into a new school year.

"And they're not my friends," she adds.

Ah. *People* = friends. Fake friends.

I wonder what they did to her.

"You want me to beat 'em up?" I ask.

Joss still doesn't look at me, but she does laugh a little.

"Made you smile," I say.

She nods.

"Can we just sit out front for lunch?" she finally asks.

"Sure," I say. "Yeah. With Gentry, or . . . ?"

"It's whatevs," she says. "He's fine."

Meet me and Joss out front for lunch, I text Gentry at the end of third period. *She's sad.*

How come? he asks.

I type *Idk* and he writes back *Cool.*

Since I know Joss doesn't want to go anywhere near the cafeteria, I dip inside to get food before meeting them on the grass out front. Between my school lunch and the feed bag Gentry's dad packed for him, at least I know we're not gonna starve.

Gentry's dad made sure to put Oreos in his lunch. Well, not real Oreos—more like the store brand. But they're not all broken up into crumbs like what Renée usually brings home. And they're not stale either.

"Hey," Gentry says, holding one up. "If you could be a cookie, what kind would you be?"

Joss looks annoyed. "Seriously? This is the question?"

But I think this is a perfect distraction for whatever's on her mind right now, so I say, "Chocolate chip. Straight out of the oven."

They both go, "Mmm," and then Gentry says, "I'd be a gooey brownie."

"I dunno," Joss tells him. "I see you more as a snickerdoodle."

I think he's a little offended.

"If I'm a snickerdoodle, you're a lemon bar."

But she doesn't even get a chance to clap back. A car squeals up to the curb in front of the school, peeling our attention away from the cookie topic. Some dude gets out of the car looking all kinds of mad. He doesn't seem to care that he's parked in the drop-off zone. He just slams the door behind him and crushes sidewalk and gravel under his feet as he chews toward the building.

He stands in front of the main office instead of going inside, takes out his phone, smash-taps something on it.

His energy makes me nervous. It reminds me too much of Jordan.

"Someone's in deep trouble," Gentry whispers. "I wonder whose dad that is."

I'm pretty sure we all do.

Something tells me we're about to find out.

Our Principal, Mrs. Blanco...

... breezes through those double doors out front like the total boss she is.

One of the counselors, Mr. Vang, is with her.

"I texted my son," the man says. "That's who I want to see."

"Come inside with me," Mrs. Blanco calmly tells him. "He's in my office."

The man steps back. "I'm *not* going inside. I want to see my son. *Now.*"

The seconds that pass before Mrs. Blanco answers are full of chirping birds and traffic going by and kids from school laughing and talking. The three of us are definitely not laughing or talking, though. We're waiting to see what happens next.

The principal nods once at Mr. Vang. He spins on the back of his shoe and goes inside.

Mrs. Blanco doesn't look at us or acknowledge anyone else is around, but she does say, "I think it would be much better if we had this conversation privately, inside my office."

"I'm not setting *one foot* in that building," the man says. "And I'll deal with my son the way I see fit."

The principal leans in and says something too quiet for us to hear.

The dad goes, "It's none of your damn business."

"It happened at school," she says. "That makes it my business."

But the man pushes past her as the double doors swing open and Mr. Vang comes back through them with . . .

Wiz Porter?

"What did you do?" his dad bellows.

People start to pool around on the grass and stare at the drama unfolding in front of school right now, right in the middle of lunch.

Wiz looks a lot smaller than normal standing in front of his dad.

"I just—"

"You took *my stuff*?" Mr. Porter yells. "And then you were stupid enough to get *caught* with it."

Wiz stares at the ground without moving. Which is weird, because his dad can't stop moving.

"What kind of an idiot would do that? Huh?" He's pacing side to side now, like he's shadowboxing with Wiz. "How do you think you got that Xbox? And those clothes?" He flips the strings of Wiz's hoodie. They hit him in the face, but Wiz doesn't so much as twitch.

Mrs. Blanco eases in, says something I can't hear. Mr. Vang looks like he's ready to pounce, too, but Wiz's dad pushes them both away. Like the only thing he can see through the firewall of his rage is his son.

Wiz is concrete. His dad can't get any sort of reaction out of him, so he just starts pacing faster, and faster, until something seems to break inside him. He pushes within an inch or two of his son and shouts, "*Why the hell would you do that?*"

To all our surprise, Wiz straightens up. His face gets hard—not smirky hard the way it does in class, but some other kind of hard. Like he's challenging his own father.

"*I asked you a question!*" Mr. Porter huffs.

"Because I didn't want you to go to jail again!" Wiz shouts.

Mr. Porter lunges for his son, connects a few times against Wiz's head with his open hand as Mrs. Blanco and Mr. Vang jump right in to protect him. I'm not sure who called for the school resource officers to come, but in almost no time, there are cops everywhere. Only they don't go after Wiz. They swarm his dad. Before we can process it all, Mr. Porter is on the ground in handcuffs. Mrs. Blanco says something quiet to one of the cops, but we can't hear that, either, even though the three of us are staring, practically leaning in their direction.

That's when Wiz sees us.

He looks . . . humiliated.

Mrs. Blanco puts her hand on Wiz's shoulder. She leans in and asks him something, and even though he's looking straight down at the ground, he nods, his face patchy red. As they take Mr. Porter away, I realize . . . Wiz isn't the one who's in trouble. It's his dad. His *dad* was doing something bad.

One of the cops tells the principal, "We'd like to get a statement from the son, but for now why don't you go ahead and take him inside?"

Mrs. Blanco nods, and Mr. Vang puts his arm protectively around Wiz's shoulders. Before we know it, the cops take Mr. Porter away, and now that the show is over, the crowd that had gathered to watch is gone too.

Me and Gentry and Joss turn back toward each other with our mouths hanging all the way open. It feels a little like I'm watching a movie about the night my mom got arrested. Or about every first night at a new foster home. About the terrifying unknown of what's going to happen next. Or the equally terrifying unknown of why things went down the way they did. If they're taking Mr. Porter to jail, it probably means he has a record. Which could mean he's hurt Wiz before, or someone else. Or he already has drug charges against him. One thing's for sure. Whatever it is, Wiz has had to live with it every single day.

Joss finally says, "So do we think Wiz uses all that Axe to cover up the smell of his *dad's* pot?"

Her words hit my stomach like a ninety-mile-an-hour

baseball, because that's what I've been thinking too. "Yeah," I say. "His dad's the one in trouble. Not him."

Gentry asks, "How do you do that to your own kid, though?"

"How could I do that to Wiz?" I whisper.

They turn and stare at me.

"What do you mean?" Gentry asks. "Do what?"

I look over, to the spot on the sidewalk where Wiz Porter stood up to his dad and revealed a horrible truth. Not about him, or his dad, or his family.

But about me.

About how I made fun of Wiz for being a stoner, when I didn't know a single thing about his actual life. How it wasn't him growing, selling, or smoking pot. It was his dad. He was covering up the smell of what his *dad* was doing. And Wiz was still so worried about protecting his old man, he was willing to risk himself.

I don't answer Gentry's question, and he doesn't push me to. We just sit there. Me. And Joss. And Gentry. Staring down at our shoes. Or the grass. Or the sidewalk.

We don't say another word to each other until the bell rings for lunch to be over.

I wish this whole horrible day would be over too.

But it's not.

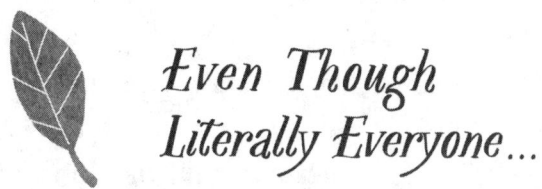

Even Though Literally Everyone...

...is talking about what happened at lunch, Mrs. Duncan acts like nothing's different. It's just another basic day in math class.

But not in PE.

Coach has us sit in the bleachers instead of down on the gym floor, like we usually do before our warm-ups. She's wheeled out a plastic cart, the kind the science teachers use to hold beakers and stuff. Only Coach's cart has a giant, empty pickle jar on top and four plastic containers on the shelf down below.

Coach scans the bleachers for a second.

"Taryn," she says. "Come on down here."

Several kids shout, "You're the next contestant on *The Price Is Right*!"

Coach smiles as she pulls one of the containers up from the bottom shelf and puts it next to the pickle jar.

Taryn peeks inside.

Coach says, "Your job is to put the items from this plastic container into the jar."

"All of them?" Taryn asks.

"Whatever can fit."

Taryn reaches into the plastic tub and takes out a tennis ball. She drops it into the pickle jar, then reaches for another tennis ball, then another. She manages to get about six into the jar.

"Why'd you stop?" Coach asks.

"There's no more room," Taryn says. "It's full."

"You're telling me nothing else will fit in the jar," Coach says.

"Um . . . yeah?"

"Thank you. You may be seated. Evan?"

As Evan Otoshi comes down from the stands, Coach swaps out plastic containers.

"Can *you* fit anything else inside the jar?" she asks.

Evan reaches into the container, takes out as many ping-pong balls as he can hold, and starts dropping and pushing them into the spaces around the tennis balls. Some of them get dented as he jams them in, but Coach just says, "That's okay. Keep going."

Soon it looks like all the empty spaces are filled up with ping-pong balls.

But Coach calls another girl down from the bleachers and hands her what turns out to be a container of marbles, and that girl dumps a bunch of marbles into the jar. They shimmy down into all the bitty spaces between tennis balls and ping-pong balls.

Coach stands there, looking pretty satisfied with the pickle jar.

"Is it full now?" she asks.

Some people shout yes and some shout no, but I raise my hand.

"Ash?"

"There's spaces we can't even see," I tell her, but the rest of the class is so caught up in the full-versus-not-full debate, my words get lost in all the noise.

It takes a minute for Coach to shush everyone.

"Say it again, Ash," she says.

I clear my throat. "There's still some tiny spaces we can barely see."

Coach keeps her eyes on me as she tips her head toward the cart where the pickle jar is, and I get up slowly and make my way down. She holds the last container out to me.

"Can you fill those spaces?"

I look at her without moving, and she nods, signaling me to take the container.

I slip it out of her hands. It's smaller than the others, but heavy. I'm the only one who can see what's inside it until I pour the contents into the jar, which I finally do.

The sand fills up every molecule of empty space around the rest of the contents as the rest of the class mumbles and says things like "I knew she was gonna do that!" and "Oh, wow!" and "That's so cringe!"

As I climb back into the bleachers, Matt Adams calls out, "What's that supposed to prove?"

"It's not really meant to *prove* anything," Coach says. "But . . . let's pretend that the tennis balls were something else. Let's pretend they're rumors floating around school, for example. Maybe about someone's grades, or who's dating who, or—" She pauses for a second while the class giggles. "Or things about someone's family. Anything like that." She points to the jar. "If we'd stopped the experiment after just putting the tennis balls in, we would have left class believing the jar was already full. We all saw it, right? No more tennis balls would fit. If we stop listening after we hear a rumor, we might come to the same conclusion. But there's always more. More details. More truth. Things we can't see because we believe that what we *can* see is all that's there."

The thought makes my chest ache. I'm not sure if this is about Wiz or something else instead. Or maybe everything else. But I'm listening close. And I'm not the only one.

"The thing about rumors," Coach says, "is that even when we think we've seen something with our very own eyes, it often turns out to only be part of a bigger story. So, while this experiment wasn't meant to prove anything"—she looks at Matt when she says this—"I hope it can be a pause before deciding to spread or even believe a rumor. No matter who you hear the rumor from."

I decide to skip the locker-room part at the end of class and go up to Coach Miller instead.

"Need help?" I ask.

Coach looks at me for a second.

"Sure," she says.

We start to separate out the contents of the jar.

"Sometimes it's the same for people," I say.

"Yeah?" She shakes the sand off the last tennis ball before putting it in its container. "Tell me more about that."

"Sometimes . . . it's like . . . everyone else only sees the tennis balls, but there's all this . . . sand around everything. Like, details people can't see. About your life."

"That sounds about right," she says.

After the ping-pong balls are out, we use our fingers to sift out the marbles and put them back in their container.

"How come it's so hard for people to see the sand and not just the tennis balls?" I ask.

"Oh, that's a good question," Coach says. "I think sometimes it helps to let people know about the sand. That it's there. What it looks like. You know?"

I walk with her as she wheels the cart back to her office, and when we get there, she turns to me.

"What would you want someone to know about your sand?" she asks.

I clear my throat.

"I . . ."

Coach sits down on the edge of the desk and waits.

"I don't . . ."

She leans forward. "What is it, Ash? What's going on?"

My heart feels like a trapped squirrel, bouncing off the words stuck inside my chest. I don't know how to say it.

"I can't go home tonight," I blurt.

For the first time since school started, her chill seems like it's about to crack.

"What do you mean?"

"I . . . I got kicked out of my house. Well, not kicked out, but . . . I was told not to come back tonight, because Jordan needed some cooling-off time."

"Jordan is your—?"

"My foster mom's . . . son. She says to think of him like my uncle, but he's—" I stop myself before saying he's not supposed to be there.

She nods. "What does he need cooling-off time for?"

"Because otherwise, Gladys, my foster mom, is afraid he would hurt me."

Coach closes her eyes for a split second.

Somewhere in another part of the gym, a phone rings.

"Have you shared any of this with . . . anyone?" she asks.

I say, "Gladys doesn't like me talking about family business. She told me not to."

The look on her face is starting to freak me out, so I backpedal. "It's not a big deal. I was going to ask Gentry if I could stay at his house tonight, but he's in ACE right now."

Coach stands up.

"Let's take you to ACE, then," she says. "You can hang out with Gentry, but you have to promise me you'll stay there until I come back, okay?"

"Okay."

Coach locks up her office and walks with me to the 500 wing.

Part of me feels nervous about what will happen when Gladys and Jordan find out I told on them.

But part of me feels not-nervous.

Like maybe, finally, I did the right thing by telling.

When We Get to ACE...

...Coach Miller leans in and whispers something to Mr. Yuan. He nods and gets up from his desk.

I look around the room, spot Gentry at the Shattered! table. His attention seems split between me and whatever's going on in the game right now.

"Hey, Ash," Mr. Yuan says. "Come here. I want to show you something."

I follow him to a pair of desks that are rotated face-to-face, then look over at Gentry again. But he's gotten absorbed back into the game, it seems like.

"Shattered! can be intimidating to watch," Mr. Yuan says. "But when you learn how to play, it's actually pretty simple. Can I show you how it works?"

It takes me a second to decide if I even want to, but I guess it's okay. I mean, I'm here. What else am I going to do?

For the next half hour or so, Mr. Yuan shows me

the basic rules of the card game that Gentry and his ACE friends are so obsessed with. They call over to him every so often, talking smack and challenging him to future playoffs. He claps right back at them, then keeps on showing me how to play without even a hiccup.

I have to admit, it's pretty fun once it gets going.

When Mr. Yuan figures I can handle playing for real, I pick up my backpack so I can go join Gentry and the rest of the crew. That's when the door opens and Coach Miller walks back through it. She waves me over and we step outside.

"Because Mr. Noble is on your approved list, I checked to see if you could stay there tonight, and it's okay. So when he comes to pick up Gentry, you go with him."

I nod, noticing how sore my throat suddenly is, how sting-y my eyes are, and I beg myself not to cry. I don't care if Coach sees me, I just don't want the kids in ACE to.

"I have to tell you something else, Ash," she says, and suddenly I feel like a tire with a nail through it and the air wheezing out. "You need to know that someone from Children's Services is on their way to your foster home right now to make an assessment."

The air whooshes out of the whole rest of my body.

"*Why?*" I ask.

"I know that's probably scary," she says. "But if it's not safe, we don't want you there."

"It won't matter," I say, taking a step backward. "They just hide everything from my caseworker and lie about it, and nothing ever happens."

"It won't be like that—"

"*No!* You don't get it!"

Coach reaches out to me, but I swing away.

"My caseworker doesn't see what's real. They always know when she's coming, and I'm supposed to tell her everything's fine so she'll decide everything *is* fine, and if I have to go back to Gladys's, I'll be in *so* much trouble."

I know I'm talking loud enough for everyone in ACE to probably hear me, but I don't care anymore. She shouldn't have told anyone. *I* shouldn't have told anyone.

"Ash."

"No!" There will never be another family like the Silvas. The only place they can send me now is somewhere that's the same as Gladys's, or worse.

"You don't understand!" I scream, "*You'll never understand!*"

"Ash," Coach says again, but I don't want to hear anything she has to say. I should never have trusted her.

I run down the hall.

I run fast.

As fast as my worn-out shoes will take me.

It's probably pointless to try and outrun a PE teacher.

Luckily, Mr. Yuan ducks into the hallway to see what's going on, and in the time it takes for Coach Miller to give him the basics of the situation, I'm down the hall and out the door and squeezing through the opening in the chain-link fence.

As soon as I hit the cemetery, I scale the tree from the other day and catch my breath and wait.

I didn't know how to do this part when I was four. When the room that was supposed to be *my* room exploded because my mom and her friends were cooking meth behind the closed door. I just stood there in the front yard, exposed, watching our house burn, not knowing how sad my life was about to become once they took my mom away, and then me.

But that was the one and only time I ever let things happen that way. And now . . . ?

I've gotten really good at hiding and waiting for the scary part to be over.

Once I'm up the Tree...

...I can't hold back the flood of tears anymore. I don't make any noise. I learned how to silent-cry long before living with Gladys, but knowing how sure didn't hurt once Jordan moved in, considering how much he *hates* when people cry.

I don't have anything to wipe my face with except my shirt, but whatever. It doesn't even matter. Nothing matters.

I dig into my bag, fish out my sketchbook. Through hot tears and snot, I draw Drago rage-venting as crowds of people cower from her in fear. No one messes with Drago, especially when she's mad. Her anger is a worldwide phenomenon. Newspaper headlines warn the masses not to intervene: DRAGO IS THE FRIEND YOU DON'T WANT AS AN ENEMY.

I'm just about to put an axe in Drago's hand so she can exact her revenge on the worst evildoers on the planet when I hear a familiar *click-click* below me.

I know it's Joss without even looking.

I wait for the sound of her skateboard to pass by on her way to her grandma's grave, but it doesn't. It stops. Right below me.

I hold my breath.

"I knew you'd be here," Joss calls up the tree to me.

I grab the bottom of my T-shirt and wipe off my face real quick.

"No, you didn't."

"Did too."

"How?" I ask.

"Because I saw you the other day. When you were spying on me."

"I wasn't spying on you," I say, wishing she'd just say *Okay* and move on. I kind of want to be alone right now.

But she doesn't. She puts her skateboard and bag down on the grass under the tree and starts to climb.

"*What are you doing?*" I ask.

"What's it look like?" she says from halfway up.

"I didn't invite you," I say.

"It's a public tree. I don't need to be invited."

I slam my sketchbook closed and shove it into my backpack. She doesn't ask what I'm doing or what I'm drawing like I expect her to. She doesn't ask anything. Just straddles the tree limb next to me. The air up here is a confusing mix of tree bark and car fumes and the sound of the drive-through speakers drifting over from the McDonald's across the street. I don't even notice how hot my face feels until a breeze kicks up and blows against it.

"They're freaking out about you at school right now," she finally says.

I'm not surprised, but I don't tell her that. Joss left her bag and board under this tree, which means if they come looking for me here, I'll be easy to find. That's all I can think about right now.

"Coach Miller asked if I knew where you were," she says.

That gets my attention. I want to know what she told Coach, but I don't ask. I just stare at her.

"If you even care," she says, tossing her hair over her shoulders, "I told her I see you at Dutch Bros by the skate park after school, like, all the time."

That Dutch Bros is way the other direction from the cemetery.

"You did?"

She nods. "Just to prove it, I told her you usually get the Unicorn Blood."

Details. Sand.

I let my breath out finally.

"So, why'd you bolt, anyway?" she asks.

"Did you see Gentry?"

"Yeah."

"But . . . you didn't tell him where I was?"

"I didn't know where you were. I just guessed. So, no."

Good. But I'm still skep.

"Why didn't you say anything to him?" I ask.

She dangles her feet for a minute, then pulls them into a crisscross, holding on to some smaller branches to help keep her steady.

"I figured if you wanted him to know anything, you would have told him yourself."

It's not that I *don't* want Gentry to know where I am. I'm just afraid he would have tried to find me, and they would have followed him. He's not that stealth.

I'm glad Joss didn't snitch on me, but that still doesn't mean I want her here. I don't, for a whole bunch of reasons.

"So why *did* you bolt?" she asks again.

That's one of the reasons.

I don't want to talk about it.

"Why didn't you tell me you saw me here the other day?" I ask instead.

"Sometimes people just need their privacy."

Now I feel bad, because I kind of invaded *her* privacy by spying on her, then going to look at her grandma's grave.

I'm not even out of that thought before another one takes over.

"Why didn't you want to sit in the cafeteria today?" I ask.

Joss swings her eyeline in my direction. "Because my so-called friends are homophobic jerks."

My face feels hot all over again. "Did they say something about me?"

Joss pretend-laughs and shakes her head, but she doesn't answer.

"Did they? It's okay if you tell me. I'm used to—"

"Kendalyn Meyer saw a picture of my family online, and . . . they were making fun of *me*, Ash. Not you. Me."

"*You?* But you're not . . . you're not . . ."

I don't know how to finish the sentence. I know she likes Gentry—

Joss pulls her phone out, taps and swipes a few times, then flips the screen around to show me.

"My papa Alex tagged me without thinking about it. And my papa Joaquín didn't catch it until it was too late."

I stare at the photo. Of Joss. Joss and her dads. They look happy. They look like a family, like the kind of family everyone wants. Kicking it somewhere cool, maybe on vacation, laughing and having fun with each other. They look nice like the Silvas, just with two dads instead of a dad and a mom.

"When we moved here, I asked them not to tag me or show my face in their pictures," she says. "It's not that I don't love them. I do. I love them tons. But I know how people are."

I keep staring at the photo until she pulls it away.

"They love me too. They say they're so proud of me, it's hard not to post about what a great kid I am. I know it hurts their feelings, but . . . They've taught me about boundaries and consent my whole life, and . . . they're usually really good about, like, practicing it."

The sound of traffic and the McDonald's drive-through and the birds chirping all warp together in my head like some creepy clown movie. Why would she keep that a secret from us—from me? Or Gentry? We wouldn't care. I mean, God, she has two parents who love her and are proud of her and who take her places. I hate that she's so afraid of people giving her crap for it, she'd rather keep her family such a gigantic secret.

"I would never make fun of you for having two dads," I whisper.

"I know." She nods but looks away. "It's not just that people make fun, though, Ash. It's . . . People say a lot of hateful, horrible things about us. Like how we're not a *real* family." She uses air quotes around that word. "Or how my dads are going to hell. How I should be taken away from them and put up for adoption."

I don't even know what to say to that.

"Like being adopted when I'm twelve would be better for me than my actual, real family, just because at least then I'd have a dad and a mom. As if that's the only thing that makes a family *good*."

"I'm in foster care," I blurt. "And my foster family is . . ." I look at her because I can't believe I'm telling her this. "They're not a good family. They're not even good people."

Joss finally looks at me.

"That's why I'm in this tree right now. I told Coach Miller something private, and she went and told the school, and now they're going to make a big deal out of it."

"Seriously . . . ?" She looks toward school, then back again. "Why didn't you say something to me before?"

"Because there's nothing to say. No one cares. They're just going to send me back to my foster mom and everything will be worse than it was."

"So . . . what if you *don't* go back?" Joss asks.

My side-eye turns into full-frontal eye. "What do you mean?"

"I mean . . . what if you refuse to go back?"

I don't know how to answer her. It sounds great, except . . . I'm pretty sure it doesn't work that way.

"You could stay with us," she says while I'm still thinking about it. "And I know Gentry's dad would let you stay there—he's so nice, and he totally likes you. It's a dead giveaway—if the parents like you, they bring you snacks. If they don't, it means they're so anxious for you to leave, they don't want you to even get comfortable."

I laugh a little, just barely, just one of those laughs that blows through your nostrils.

Joss takes her phone out again and taps out a message. A reply pings back almost immediately.

"My papa Joaquín's on his way to come get us," she says.

"I'm not allowed to go with anyone who's not on the list—"

"Well, you can't stay up in this tree forever. Don't worry. He'll know how to fix it. He can fix anything."

A few minutes later, Joss spies her dad pulling into the cemetery. We shimmy down the tree and make a run for it, just in case Coach Miller and Mr. Yuan are still looking for me.

Sitting in the back seat of Joss's dad's SUV, I think about Gentry—how I was supposed to stay at his house tonight. He's probably worried. I should definitely let him and Sam know I'm safe.

I pull out my phone.

Hey. I'm okay, I write.

The answer comes back in a flash.

For real?

For real. Let your dad know, okay?

I stick my phone back in my pocket and watch out the window as the pieces of Joss's kaleidoscope life start to come together.

Joss Lives in a Really Nice House...

...**in the Avenues.** Her papa Joaquín calls it "Spanish style."

He says, "I love a good Spanish style. That white stucco with the rounded redbrick roof. And of course, all those wrought-iron details and archways everywhere—I love that aesthetic."

"Don't get him started," Joss fake-whispers to me. "He can literally talk about this stuff all day."

Her dad does like to talk, but at least he's talking and not yelling, so there's something comforting about the way he chatters.

Joss's other dad is already home when we get there. Her dads look like guys you'd see in a magazine—not for fashion, but like... for house decorating. Or cooking. It smells like food in the house, like someone's actually cooking real food.

My stomach rumbles.

"Ash, this is my husband," her papa Joaquín says, signaling toward the man in an apron coming from the kitchen.

"Alex," that dad says. "*He/him.*"

"Oh," I say. "Um. Ash. *She/her.*"

"I know we have some things to talk about," Joaquín says to me. "Figure out what's up and how best to handle it. But let's get you settled while we finish dinner."

I can't get over how much Joss looks like her papa Joaquín. Like, copy/paste.

Joss tugs me by the backpack strap and tells them, "Sure. We'll go play video games while you two adult-talk." She uses air quotes again.

My head spins. I feel like I'm in a TV show as Joss takes me down the hall to her room. When we get there, she slips my backpack from me and tosses it on one of two narrow beds. I sneak a look around at the walls plastered in skateboard and surf posters, a bookcase full of medals and trophies and plushies. The wall by the door is covered in skateboards that look like shelves, only they're not. They're just perched on top of pegs sticking out of the wall to make a skateboard parking lot.

"Do you actually use all those?" I ask.

"Yup."

"Wow."

I turn to her.

"Are we really gonna play video games?"

She laughs. "Only if you want to. Or we could do homework, if you have any."

"Do *you* have any?"

She makes a funny mouth noise. "Man, I always have homework. Like, I *have* to finish my family tree for social studies. I started it late, and it's due tomorrow."

As soon as she says it, for the first time since Mr. Mann gave us that cringe assignment, I start to have an idea. Maybe I *can* turn in a family tree project tomorrow. I unzip my backpack, pull out my clothes and one or two notebooks before I find my good pencils down at the bottom. I know he said he'd give extra credit if our presentations were digital, but . . . that's not my superpower. Drawing is.

I open the notebook and start to sketch.

Alex knocks on the door a while later.

"Dinner," he says.

When we get to the dining room, the table is set up all nice, with dishes that match and aren't made out of paper, and three tall candles burning in the middle. I slow to an almost-stop the last few steps.

"This looks like a restaurant," I say before I can stop myself.

Alex smiles, and Joaquín says, "Alex definitely has the touch."

"Yeah, cuz we're so fancy," Joss says, rolling her eyes.

"Hush, tween!" Joaquín tells her, and they all kind of laugh.

I'm still standing a few feet from the table.

Joss looks at me like I'm weird.

"You can sit down," she says.

But there are six chairs around the table, and some of them have plates but some don't, and . . . I'm starting to get that frozen feeling again.

Alex jumps up and pulls out one of the chairs for me.

"Thank you," I whisper.

The food on the table looks like magazine food: a plate of chicken and sauce that's brown and bubbly and warm, plus a salad bowl with so many colors in it—not just green lettuce, but yellow peppers, red tomatoes, something purple that I don't know what it is. I've only ever seen food like this in real life at the Silvas, and that's been a while.

"We don't usually say grace," Joaquín tells me. "But we can if you'd like to."

"Oh. No. That's okay. I'm not . . . I'm good."

There's a flurry of commotion while everyone puts salad and baked chicken and potatoes on their plates. They chat as we eat, about small things. How everyone's day was. What happened at school or work. Joss tells them about Wiz Porter and makes sure I add my thoughts, since I saw what happened too.

"I feel so bad for that young man," Joaquín says, putting his hand against his chest, right where his heart is. "Can you imagine how confusing this must be for him?"

I actually can, but I'm not ready to tell them about all that.

The conversation flows from one topic to the next, like the water in Little Chico Creek after a big rain. They laugh and tease each other. No one yells or seems angry. It doesn't feel like anyone's being extra careful not to say the wrong thing. I wonder if it's like this every night at Joss's house, or if it's just a show they're putting on because I'm here.

I silently wish it's not just a show.

The conversation starts to drift as everyone finishes eating, and that's when Joaquín says, "Ash, I know things are going to get complicated for you for a while. There are a lot of moving parts to a situation like this."

"It took me seven foster homes before I felt like I was somewhere I could breathe," Alex jumps in. "I was about your age, too, but it did finally work out. Believe me when I say, I understand how hard this all is. But we're going to do everything we can to get you into the best situation."

My face goes tingly. Joss's dad was in foster care? Why didn't she tell me about her papa Alex when we were up in the tree? Because him being in foster care would mean he actually does understand. I'm even starting to think Joaquín really can help fix this, like

Joss said. And that feels like letting out a deep breath I didn't know I was holding. Like maybe her dads could be someone to believe in.

After dinner, I help her clear the dishes and put the leftovers away, while her dads go into the living room, start making phone calls and strategizing how to deal with everything.

When we're done, Joss tells them, "We're gonna go work on that big assignment for tomorrow."

Alex goes, "Is it the family tree project?"

"Yup."

"Ash, are you good?" Alex asks. "Need any help, or . . . ?"

"Um. No? I think I'm solid."

"Okay, well, let me know if either of you needs anything. Markers. Snacks. Whatevs."

Joaquín goes, "*Whatevs?*"

"Isn't that what the cool kids are saying now?" Alex laughs. "Look at me—I'm cool again!"

"Sweetheart, you were never cool."

They giggle like *they're* in middle school.

Joss rolls her eyes. "You guys are so gross."

"Tween, please," Joaquín says. "Go. Do your homework. Crush that family tree."

We go back to Joss's room and get to work. We hardly talk to each other. Joss does her thing on the computer, importing images of famous people into her document so she can squeeze Mr. Mann for every last extra-credit point possible.

I'm not doing any of that.

I'm sticking to what I know.

Just me, a pen, and a sheet of paper that's been nothing but blank.

Until now.

 # *I Have No Idea...*

...what's going to happen when I get to school in the morning. If my caseworker will be there. If I'm going to get in trouble for staying at the Cruzes' last night. Or if Joss's dads are.

So far, the only thing that's anything is the way everyone's staring at Wiz Porter.

Half the school is whispering about him, too, without even trying to "hide their obvious," like Gentry says. It feels strange. I'm used to people doing that to me, since I've been the weird kid everywhere I've lived. But now they're doing it to Wiz because of his dad getting arrested in front of school yesterday. It's so pointless.

In second period, he plops onto the stool next to me, staring at the ground just like he did yesterday after they took his dad away. He doesn't look at me, doesn't say one single word, not even as we work on our experiment.

I seriously think about telling him I get it. That my mom got taken to jail right in front of me too.

That she's in prison now, and we don't know how long she'll be in this time. That she made so many bad choices while trying the best she knew how. That she did love me, and she could have seriously hurt me, and that those two facts can both be true. But . . . maybe I shouldn't say anything to Wiz. Maybe it's enough just to understand what he's going through, since I'm not the kind of person who would make him feel bad about it.

I look over at him again, at his face that somehow looks different today than it did yesterday, and decide it's *not* enough. How would he know anyone understands what he's going through unless they tell him? Unless *I* tell him.

"You probably don't know this," I say in an almost whisper. "And maybe you don't care. But . . . something like that happened with my mom too."

Only his eyes move. They slide in my direction.

"It sucks," I say. "I'm sorry you're going through that."

He stares at me for what feels like a really long time. Then he goes, "Okay."

I nod, and he nods, and for a second, we feel like two separate bits of matter occupying the same space. And then we split again, go back to our own little corner of the petri dish. Only now it feels like there may be some teensy thread still connecting us.

We have next period together, too, but Wiz makes

sure to walk far enough behind me that I can't just turn around and talk to him, even if I wanted to.

When I get to English, Ms. Kim calls me over to her desk. I'm not thinking about why, only that I just got here, and I haven't done anything to be in trouble about yet.

"Can you stay after class for a minute?" she asks.

I know I'm supposed to say yes when a teacher asks that, but today is literally the worst day for me to go late to social studies.

"I have a really big project next period," I say. "I kinda don't want to be late."

She nods. "That's fair. What about after school? Can you swing by then?"

I almost ask her why, but I don't. If it's something bad, I don't want it in my head before my presentation. I'm nervous enough about going in front of the class, and bad news can grow roots in your brain that crack a person's concentration right in half.

Instead, I just say, "Sure," and try to put it out of my mind.

During sustained silent reading time, I'm silently practicing my presentation. I wrote it out last night, but I haven't had a chance to memorize it all the way. The picture I drew to go along with it is supposed to help me remember what I want to say.

When the bell rings for fourth period, my heart body-slams my rib cage. Maybe I'll just skip it and take the F. If I give my presentation, Steven Tyler and Chase Williams are going to be there, watching me. Probably snickering and laughing and making fun. Or passing around the family tree *they* made for me. They'll find out all kinds of personal things about my life and use it against me. I bet they don't even feel sorry about what happened to Wiz Porter. Honestly, I don't know why he was ever friends with them in the first place—they're always so mean to him, especially about the whole wizard thing. Maybe he needed to feel like a wizard as a way of dealing with his dad. I bet Chase and Steven Tyler never think about how people could spread rumors about *them* just as easy as they do with people like Wiz or me.

By the time I walk into the room, I've made up my mind not to do the presentation. That's when I see Joss. I ask the person who sits next to her if we could switch seats—it's not like Mr. Mann cares, anyway. She goes, "Sure," and swings her backpack under my desk before trading with me.

"You ready?" Joss asks.

I shake my head.

"What do you mean?"

"I'm not gonna do it," I whisper.

The way she says "*Why?*" makes me feel a whole different kind of bad than the bad I felt thinking about Chase and Steven Tyler watching me.

I must have flicked a look in their direction because Joss goes, "Those guys?"

I switch back to her.

"Don't look at them," she says. "Look at me. I got you. I won't feed you to the bears, I promise." When I still don't say anything, she winks and goes, "A friend wouldn't do that to another friend."

I'm still not sure, though, even after the bell rings. To make matters worse, Mr. Mann uses a random electronic generator to pick who has to go next, instead of letting us go when we feel ready. That's bull, if you ask me.

Joss's name comes up before mine. I already know what's about to happen, because even though I was too shy to practice mine with her, she practiced hers on me last night, and it's freaking genius.

She starts her presentation by stating:

"All relationships on my family tree are accurate, but the names and faces have been altered to protect the innocent."

She's used famous skaters and surfers in place of actual family pictures and labeled them things like *Parental Unit 1* and *Parental Unit 2*. And it only shows their feet—two pairs of skater shoes on two different decks representing her dads, with a set of baby feet on a teensy skateboard just below them for herself. Her abuela is on there too. Joss told me last night: She's Alex's mom.

When she's done, Mr. Mann says, "Clap," like he does after every presentation, and as soon as the applause dies down, he says, "Thank you, Joss," before hitting the random name generator again.

I keep watching the clock. Mr. Mann told us we wouldn't get to everyone on the first day. Now I just pray my name won't come up, that we'll run out of time, and I'll get an extra day before—

Ash Dalton

There it is. My name, up on the smartboard for everyone to see.

It says *Ash*. Not Ashley.

Mr. Mann must have changed it in the computer.

I take it as a sign—a good omen.

I'm going to do it.

I'm really going to give my family tree presentation in front of Chase and Steven Tyler and Mr. Mann and everyone.

It Feels Like It Takes Twenty Minutes...

...to walk to the front of the class. Like the floor is quicksand and I have to unstick my feet with each step before taking the next one.

"Are you using the computer?" Mr. Mann asks, since everyone else has pulled their project up from their school account.

I shake my head.

The paper in my hand seems awkward all of a sudden, like it's not enough. Like it's amateur hour compared with all the slick presentations the rest of the class is doing.

I look over at Joss. She makes a face like *You got this.*

I wish I was brave like her.

I have a death grip on my picture. It's a 3D drawing of a tree trunk, with the cross section of the stump clearly visible. I started drawing it at Joss's yesterday. The words came to me last night as we were sitting there at a real dinner table with real food and a family that feels real, even if some people don't think it is because there's two dads and no mom.

"I don't have a family tree," I say, wishing I could make my voice and hands stop shaking. "Not like most of yours. I have this." I hold the paper up. "Trees . . . um . . . have bark on the outside. So, like . . . all walnut trees have the same kind of bark, which is different than the bark of a peach tree, or an almond tree."

I stop to take a breath, and someone quietly corrects my pronunciation of *almond*. That seems to be an ongoing argument in this town, but I try not to let it throw me.

"What I mean is . . . sometimes you can look at the . . . bark? And tell what kind of tree it is. But . . . the only way to know the *story* of a tree is . . . by looking at the rings inside."

I trace the circles on the stump, holding it higher so everyone can see.

"Trees don't have all their rings when they first start out. They . . . add a new one every year. And each ring? Has its own story to tell. About what was going on around that tree as it was growing up."

I glance around the room. Everyone looks confused or bored, and suddenly my face feels clammy. I look over at Joss. She's smiling—not like she's making fun. Not at all.

I clear my throat. "I guess what I'm trying to say is, roots and branches aren't the only important parts of a . . . of a tree. The rings are important too. Just as important as the roots or branches or . . . or bark. Maybe even more, because . . . it's more of, like . . . who we are inside. And . . . it's the same with families. Like, not all families are what they look like on the outside. Some parents get divorced." I follow the rings with my finger as I say this. "Or they never get married to start with. Or someone gets sick. Or dies. Or they have to take care of their parents when *they* get old. Or they can't raise the kids they have, and those kids go into foster care or get adopted." I clear my throat again, but I can't stop the ringing in my ears as I quickly decide whether to say the next part the way I wrote it down. I take another deep breath. "My mom couldn't take care of me. And I went into foster care. It hasn't always worked out great, but . . . I think it will . . . someday. I just think, if the people you're with . . . if they love each other . . . if they're good to each other . . . if they care about making sure you're always okay . . . then a family like mine, that's made up of rings instead of roots and branches, is just as good as any other kind of family, and . . ."

 I look up at Mr. Mann. He's leaning on his elbows, with his fingers pressed against his lips. Maybe he's just concentrating. Maybe he doesn't mean to, but it looks like he's frowning, and I'm suddenly petrified that I failed this project.

 I stop talking and wait, but nothing happens except

the sound of the second hand on the wall clock ticking forward.

"That's all," I add before heading back to my seat.

"Clap," Mr. Mann says before thanking me and hitting the random generator again. "Taryn Swisher, you're up."

And just like that, my presentation is over.

My new caseworker, Gabi, set it up for me to go to ACE after school with Gentry. She texted me at lunch so I'd know to hang out there until she could come get me. I haven't met Gabi in person yet, but I feel like she might be okay. Like she's trying to keep some things the way they've been—at least as much as possible. She says not everything has to change just because I'm not going to live with Gladys anymore.

But before I go to ACE, I have to stop by and see Ms. Kim like I promised.

"Have a seat," she says.

I don't move.

"Am I in trouble?" I ask.

Her "No" sounds confused, but then she says it again, more convincing.

"No, Ash, of course not. I wanted to talk to you about your poem—your free write."

Oh no . . . I never even thought about that free

write once I left class because so many other things happened after that.

"I'll be honest, Ash—I was pretty worried by what you wrote. I wasn't sure if it was just a poem, or . . . or if it was something else. So I went to see your counselor."

This isn't good. At all. Once the grown-ups start talking about you, they make decisions that you don't get to be a part of, and it never works out well. Even the Silvas didn't *ask* me if I wanted to stay or if I didn't. *I'm so sorry, sweetheart*, Ana had said. Because they'd already talked it over and decided without me.

"I also had a chance to talk to Coach Miller," Ms. Kim says. "It seems that some of your other teachers have similar concerns. But I think you know that by now?"

I nod, still not sure where this is going.

"I'm glad you reached out to Coach," she says. "Hopefully this will give the people who care about you a chance to figure everything out."

"Okay," I whisper.

"I just want you to know, you've got some good people on your side, including me. It may not have always seemed that way—let's face it, it may not have always *been* that way for you. But it's that way now. Are you able to take that in and trust it?"

I nod again.

"Thanks for remembering to come by," Ms. Kim says. "Oh, and Ash?"

I'm already headed for the door, but I hold my breath and turn to look at her.

"I really hope you keep writing and drawing," she says. "You're *really* good at it. I even believed I *was* that three-headed supervillain for a minute."

She smiles, and I smile back.

Ms. Kim may be a lot of things.

But she's definitely not a villain.

When I get to ACE, Gentry deals me in on a new round of Shattered! Mr. Yuan sits in on this round too.

"I'm taking you all out," he says, pointing at each of us. "Every last one of you."

"Those are fighting words, Mr. Yuan," Mónica says.

I don't say anything. No smack talk like the rest of them, no threats of world Shattered! domination, nothing. I just concentrate on my cards and quietly play what comes up.

That's why everyone is in absolute shock when I take the whole thing. I even beat Mr. Yuan. And not because anyone let me win either. There's no way to let someone win in Shattered! Like Mr. Yuan says, the cards don't lie.

We're a couple of rounds in before I get a text that

Gabi's out front to pick me up. She messaged me again right after school just to make sure I knew the plan. That doesn't always happen. Caseworkers don't always keep you informed like that, mostly because they don't have time. Sometimes they're too busy to figure out what's really going on at all, like my last caseworker, Barbara. She didn't even know she was getting tricked on the regular by Gladys and Jordan.

"My ride's here," I say, putting my phone away. "I'm peacing out."

"Oh sure," Henry says. "It's easy to ditch after you win. No one can take you down, and you'll always be the champ."

"Don't worry," I say. "I'll come back and smoke you all again."

The sound of them riffing on each other follows me halfway down the hall.

The feeling of being part of something stays with me long after I leave.

I can tell who Gabi is as soon as I see her. She looks like someone's cool sister in college. She doesn't have that vibe of being nervous or worried or tired like other caseworkers I've seen. She's just sitting there, chilling in her sunglasses, smiling, waiting out front to take me home. Not to my real home—not yet. But she tells me she's working on that.

"What is it you really want, Ash?" she asks. "What would be the ideal situation for you?"

No one has ever asked me that before.

"I want to live with people who actually care about me," I tell her, knowing it'll probably be a deal-breaker. "And I want to stay there. Like, permanently." I'm positive she'll say what everyone else has said: *We can't promise anything, Ash, but we'll try.*

Instead, Gabi tells me, "I'll do everything in my power to make that happen."

And for the first time, I wonder if it's actually possible to have a caseworker I can believe in.

 *Friday Afternoon...*

...I get to go home with Gentry after school. His dad even kicks us some money for Dutch Bros on our way to the skate park. Joss meets us there. I guess we really are a crew now.

I wave at Joss's papa Joaquín as he drops her off. He smiles and waves back.

"What are you getting, Ash?" Joss asks as we wait at the Dutch Bros window to order.

"Unicorn Blood, duh," I say.

"Bleh." She turns to Gentry. "What about you?"

"Galaxy Fish. Why, what are you getting?"

"Dragon Slay-ah!" she says, and we all laugh because everyone knows Dragon Slayer turns your tongue blue.

Not that Joss cares, because she doesn't. When she skates the bowl at Humboldt Park, she sticks her blue tongue out as she grabs massive air and flashes rock-star hands at us.

Later, as she smokes Gentry at *Mario Kart* again, I sketch them leaning into each other as they drift.

I'm starting to think Gentry isn't as bad at *Mario Kart* as he pretends to be. I think he's actually working a whole sympathy angle with Joss, throwing the controller down in pretend fury when he "loses."

"You know what, Ash?" he says. "I think we should teach Joss how to play Shattered!, don't you?"

"For sure," I tell him. "You can't cheat at Shattered!"

Joss's jaw drops. "Are you suggesting I *cheat*?" she squeals.

"Did I say that?" I gasp.

"You implied it," Gentry adds.

"Dude." I shove against him. "Not helpful."

While Gentry gets the cards out and starts shuffling them, Joss pulls up the text message pinging in her pocket.

"It's from my papa Alex. He wanted me to know I got a ninety-five on my family tree." She rolls her eyes. "Like that couldn't have waited till later."

"Oh, come on," Gentry says, leaning into her. "You know you've been sweatin' it."

"Whatevs," she says, play-pushing him back.

My insides do a little spinout. "Hey, can I use your phone to check my Aeries?" I ask. I have my own account on the grading app, but my phone still doesn't connect to the internet.

She hands it to me, and I pull up my page.

"Holy *what*?" I shriek. "*Dude!* I got an *eighty-seven*."

I'm kind of shook.

I didn't fail.

"How'd you do on your science experiment?" Joss asks, leaning over my shoulder to see.

I find the grade and show her.

"Okay, I'm not *saying* I got an A because of Wiz," I tell them, handing the phone back to Joss. "But he didn't suck as my partner. He's actually pretty good at science."

So am I, I realize with a small zap of surprise. I've never gotten what anyone would consider "good grades" before. It's a strange feeling to be proud of myself for that.

"Dude, this is how it's gonna be when you come live with us," Joss says like it's already a fact, throwing a handful of popcorn into her mouth.

"*If* I come live with you," I correct. "Just because your dads want to take me doesn't mean they'll get to."

"Me, killing both of you at *Mario Kart* every weekend," Joss goes on, ignoring me.

"Your folks," Gentry adds. "Texting grades to both of you the whole time." He snorts, then tries to take some popcorn out of the bowl, but Joss swings it away from him. I use this move to my advantage, stealing a double handful, then going behind her back to give him some.

Joss flips around on me. "And what do you mean *if* you come live with us? Of course you will. My papa

Alex knows his way around the foster care system. And my papa Joaquín is the smartest person ever. I promise, they know what they're doing."

"Trust the process," Gentry says, nodding.

It's such a weird expression coming from him that Joss and I both freeze and stare, and suddenly he looks like he got caught stealing cookies, and that makes us both laugh.

Then he goes, "What'd I say?" and that just makes us laugh even harder.

Joss finally hands him the popcorn bowl.

"You think you'll really get to go live with Joss's family?" Gentry asks me.

"I hope so," I say as Joss cuts in with "If Children's Services knows what's good for it." She turns to me. "My papa Alex says Gabi's one of the best caseworkers he's ever met, and he would know. He feels pretty good about our chances."

I want to believe it. I do want to trust the process, like Gentry said. I want to trust people. There haven't been very many people in my life who I felt like I *could* trust, though.

I look at Joss and think, *Until now*. Which makes me smile.

Gentry switches gears, pulling Joss into an explanation of how to play Shattered!, and since I know this could go on for a while, I take out my sketchbook and pencil. But as I'm drawing them huddled over the deck of cards, Dragonia Volante begins making an unexpected appearance at the Shattered! table with us. In the background, her metal iris is wide open.

You really did vanquish all the evildoers! cartoon me says to Drago.

No, Ash, she says. *Not all. That would be impossible.*

But . . . you left your iris open. Anyone could get in here. Anyone could attack us, or . . . or hurt us . . .

True, she tells me. *But we have the strongest weapon ever.*

I look around the table, searching for a bazooka or a laser beam or a shrink ray. I don't see any kind of weapon.

There's nothing here, I tell her. *It's just us.*

Exactly, Drago says. *Us. There is nothing stronger than that.*

I sit back, stare at my sketchbook in surprise. At the talking balloons, full of more truth than I've ever seen in once place. And it came from inside *me*.

Gentry goes, "Dude. You done drawing?"

I nod.

"Can I see?" Joss asks.

I push the book toward her.

"Oh my God, Ash . . . this is *amazing*. Seriously."

"All right," Gentry says, hitting the table to get our attention. "I'm dealing everyone in. Are we good to go?"

I close the sketchbook and move it aside.

"Yeah," I say. "We're definitely good to go."

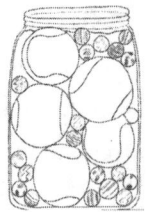 *Author's Note*

Cherished Reader,

Thank you for picking up a copy of *My So-Called Family* and spending a bit of time in Ash's world. This book is profoundly meaningful for me, and I hope it will be for you as well. Sometimes a book like this might land in a deep-feeling place, and that's okay. We can be good to ourselves in the midst of hard things.

I wrote this book, in part, because I was a schoolteacher for many years, and I knew many Ashes, Gentrys, Josses, and even Wizes. I always spent extra time with those students between classes, at lunch, and after school. Maybe it was the teacher and mom in me, but I chose to be a safe place for kids who didn't always have a trusted adult in their lives.

But I also wrote this book because, in many ways, I was a kid like Ash. I was never in foster care, but there were many ways in which my life was unsafe and unhealthy. Had there been caring, attentive adults in my world, it's possible someone would have intervened on my behalf and removed me from my harmful situation. So while Ash Dalton isn't an autobiographical version of my younger self, there is a lot of me in her, and I was able to heal some of my childhood hurt by writing her experience.

Because I hadn't personally spent time in the foster care system, I invited members of the foster care community into conversation to ensure that Ash's experience, while fictitious, was told in a truthful way. These experts are folks who live in Chico, California, where this story takes place, so their knowledge and expertise matches the experience of youth in foster care who live and go to school in that area.

While I'm on the subject of accuracy . . . for those readers who live and/or go to school in the places depicted in this story, please know that some of the details were altered for the purposes of fiction. Having lived in Chico for nearly forty years, please know I acknowledge your reality.

Sometimes when we read a book like this, emotions can come up that are tricky to manage. It might help to draw or write about it like Ash did. Talking about it can also help. A friend or trusted adult will listen to what we're going through and offer advice if we want it. Oftentimes, when we express our fears and worries out loud, it helps take away their power over us.

Whatever your situation, and whoever you call family, always remember there is a place in this world for you. You contain rings, and roots, and branches. You are your own unique story.

With all kindness,
Gia

Resources: One thing I learned in consulting with those knowledgeable with the foster care system is that the system works differently from state to state and region to region. Please consult your local agencies or school personnel for help, information, or concerns you may have—whether for yourself, a friend, or a child in your life.

Acknowledgments

To young readers everywhere—you are enough. You are whole. You are worthy of love and deserving of support. It's okay to reach out, to see who's there for you, to ask for help, to offer to help, to be a friend, to be an ally even to those you don't call friend. Your existence matters, and I'm so grateful you're here.

My gratitude to my agent, Erin Murphy, goes so far beyond *thank you*, there are no adequate words.

Supreme gratitude to my editor, Joy Peskin—it's been nothing short of a dream to work with you. Further thanks to the entire team at FSG BYR.

To cover designer Julia Bianchi and cover artist Julia Rose Barnes, for capturing Ash's world in a way that's both succinct and beautiful.

Unbound gratitude to my early readers, beta readers, and expert readers for your thoughtful and sensitive ideas, notes, suggestions, and guidance. This book would not exist if not for you: Amanda Sorg, Autumn

Brock, Doug Marshall, Jennifer Salas, Pat Zeitlow Miller, and Tami Ritter.

To librarians, booksellers, and educators—you are the true superhumans, the rock stars, the freedom fighters. We owe you the world.

To anyone who answered my Facebook research questions—you're in here too!

To my friends and found family—my rings. I'm so honored to have you in my life:

Jennifer Salas, mi hermana querida; Jorge Salas; Adriana and Alicia Salas; Naheed Hasnat; Leigh Purtill; Amy King; Doug Marshall; Kimberly Nicole Woods-Bonéy; Sally Derby; G. Neri; Elly Swartz; the Struyf family: Kurt, Ayden, Espi, and Anouk; Dave, Tanya, and Mel Bartlett; and Erica Scott. And to the memory of my friend Margaret Speaker Yuan.

To my sweet daddy-o, who always saw me and met me exactly where I was. Your memory will forever be a blessing.

To my beautiful mamacita, Frances Gordon, who took me in and showed me what unconditional love can really look like.

And to E—my rings, my roots, and all my branches.